THE OWL'S EYE

EVA GRACE

SNOWRIDGE PRESS

Published by SnowRidge Press

Cover Illustration by Sarah Moustafa

Cover Design by Dragon Pen Designs

ISBN (paperback): 978-1-958412-37-4

Printed in the United States of America

There aren't enough swords, perhaps, to satisfy you, but this one is for you, anyway, Paul:

Wise, knowledgeable, strong, and fierce

You're a better hero than any character in this book.

Love ya.

Olympia
Atlantis
Cyren
Okenaus Sea
Poseidon
Hermes
Aphrodite
Persean Plains
Hills of the Dead
Erinyes Watch-Towers
Hephaestus

Watch-Towers of the north guard
Artemis
Amazon
Fortress
Plains of
irais
Mount
Olympus
Apollo
Inachos River
Lede River
Hestia
Hades
Inachos
Lake
Plains of
Trionas
Persephone
Demeter
Lake
Lede

PROLOGUE

Athena stole away from the throne room, slipping past the other gods without being perceived. Her golden helmet, tucked underneath her arm, glimmered in the sunlight that poured from the oculus in the center of the temple. She had always admired the building, so much so that she had inspired Roman architects to build its copy once, the Pantheon. Passing through the door, she touched her fingers to the cold marble of the wall.

"One day," she told herself.

Behind her, the other gods were arguing, as they were wont to do. It was always a contest of pride and power when they assembled and it wearied Athena to listen to. Not that she did not constantly fight with them herself; she and Ares had a particularly bitter rivalry that reared its head in council meetings, but she despised the constant bickering between Zeus and Poseidon. *The crown has already been given to Zeus,* she thought, *and there is no reason to dispute it.* Besides, when the time came for the throne to be handed to the next generation of gods, as it inevitably would, it would be Athena who would take it. And she would not permit Poseidon to stand in her way.

Her footsteps resounded across the marble floor as she made her way through the labyrinthine hallways to the courtyard, and past that to the edge of the mountain on which their temple stood. Facing west, one could see the Inachos River and the long expanse of the Persean Plains, all the way to the edge of the Hills of the Dead, where demigods who had served the gods well in life now resided in death. If Athena turned her head to the North, there was the Okenaus Sea and the Plains of Irais. The sun poured its rays onto the plains and illuminated them in gold and orange, washes of colour bright and vibrant even from the heights of Olympus. She watched as Hunters and Amazons prowled in the fields and hills, and as birds and beasts moved.

One day. One day, all of this will belong to me. The crown of the gods will rest on my head. She was Zeus' favourite child, the beloved. Neither Artemis nor Apollo would ever be offered the throne. Hera would never allow it. Ares was far too impetuous, Hermes was never present, and Hephaestus was more interested in metal than humans. Only Zeus' brothers might contest the title, and Zeus hated them far too much to capitulate.

No. When Zeus steps down, it will be I who rise up.

The sun beat down upon the goddess' dark curls as she raised her helmet and sat it upon her head. The bright metal enclosed her face, covering her nose. Her grey eyes seemed like mars against the perfectly polished gold. It brightened even more in contrast with the deep black of her hair. She remained poised on the side of the cliff overlooking Olympia for several more minutes before she was interrupted by her sister, Ares.

"Dreaming of a kingdom?" she asked.

Athena cocked her head and looked at her. "Not really. Have they come to a resolution yet?"

"No," Ares said. "They're still arguing about it. I am, of course, in support of a full-out war. The longer we delay, the more we risk being caught off-guard. Zeus underestimates the abilities of the demigods. He believes they could never muster a force impressive enough to defeat us."

"You believe he is incorrect."

Ares inclined her head. "I have seen my children, taught several of them myself. I hold no pretense. I am well aware that together, they could destroy me and my temple. Zeus has never heeded his offspring. Perhaps it is unsurprising that he does not comprehend their power."

Looking back out at Olympia, Athena hummed. "You are correct, Ares, and our father is being foolish. But he will learn his lesson in time and mend his ways, I am sure of that."

"Will you not go talk to him?"

"What would that do?"

"You might be able to convince him."

At those words, Athena laughed. Her poor sister: so brilliant a tactician, so talented a warrior, and yet not wise at all. "All I would do is rile him up, Ares. He will become more entrenched in his beliefs. Discussion does not change Zeus' mind, surely you know that. It is action that will determine his course. Once the demigods begin to appear as a real threat and the war seems imminent, Zeus will whistle a different tune, and we will be ready for battle."

"It puts us at a great disadvantage."

"We will not be waiting for his approval to begin preparations. You and I and any of the other gods who see reason will move quietly and slowly. Without alerting Zeus or worrying him with appearances of dissension, we will train our forces, gather our powers, concentrate our defenses. When the time comes and Zeus declares the war to be open, we will be ready."

"Athena, that *is* dissension. What you are proposing is to ignore the authority of our king." Ares' eyes sparkled. "You're far more devious than anyone gives you credit for. I will aid you in any way that I can."

"I hide it well," Athena said. "Were I too overt, like Artemis,

I would no longer be the favoured ear of the king. Owls are always watching and never seen, Ares. It is a talent you would do well to learn. You are often so brash that you sabotage your own efforts."

"Mhmm," Ares replied. "Sure. Regardless, are you coming back inside? I was sent to collect you– the meeting is about to be adjourned."

"I will follow behind you shortly."

"Very well." Ares turned on her heel. Her chlamys trailed behind her as she reentered the building. Athena lingered behind for a few more brief moments.

Already, there was a shift in the air of Olympia and in the power of the gods. Zeus was not so all-powerful as he believed, and his control of the mortal world was dangerously unstable. Already, she had planted her people in centers of learning throughout the world and prepared them for the inevitable wars that would soon come. No transition of power was ever peaceful. The demigods felt Zeus waning and wished to take it for themselves. Athena would be prepared to defend her father, but only in exchange for the throne herself.

One way or another, she thought, I *will end up as the empress of Olympia.*

She pulled her helmet off of her head and tucked it under her arm. Turning back to the temple, she took a decisive step forward and imagined Zeus' golden laurels on her head. It was a glorious sight. Her steps carried her back to the meeting, but by the time she arrived, it had ended, and the gods had already begun to disperse.

"Where were you?" Poseidon asked, coming upon her. Athena's eyes narrowed, glinting dangerously.

"Minding the business of my followers," she lied. "I could not put that on hold, even for a council such as this."

Poseidon huffed. "You must learn that the business of the gods is far more important than that of mortals, Athena. We should all thank Chaos that you are not our leader– you would ignore the needs of every immortal for the sake of your precious humans."

Athena's voice was steely-cold as she eyed Poseidon up and down. "You have often disobeyed the will of my father for the sake of your children, Poseidon. Your temperament has oft risked the entire existence of Olympia. Were anyone a threat to the stability of our world, it would be you. Is it not your demigod children who are heading the uprising?"

"How dare you!"

"Do not presume to tell me how I ought to conduct myself. I am the daughter of Zeus and the patroness of wisdom and battle. You are a mere shell-digger who enjoys dalliances with mermaids. After all, let's not forget who won the allegiance of the Athenians, Uncle."

Before Poseidon could answer her challenge, Athena vanished in a cloud of grey plumes. When she reappeared, it was in her personal temple, amongst her Warriors. The tall golden columns glistened with the light of torches and candles, the cold stones warmed with the presence of the goddess. An eager crowd of Warriors stopped their work, put down their books, and crowded around her.

"What news from Olympus?" they asked.

"War is coming," Athena said. "I have seen it."

CHAPTER 1
ROME, ITALY

Day 1

The Pantheon lay tucked between two streets of regular housing, white brick turned pink and red by the setting sun. The fountain in front of it, with its tall Egyptian obelisk, obscured Alexandria's view as she leaned back in the rickety chair at the restaurant and sipped a limoncello. If she moved her gaze to the left of the obelisk, she could see Triniya and Jasmin taking pictures together against a small tourist shop. Turning to the right, she saw Brites and Wen-Tang with their cups of gelato. They had been there since the early afternoon, a few hours ago, and there had been no sign of Athena or any of her warriors. Not that Alexandria knew what any of them looked like– the other heroes had met them, worked with them, fought against them over the years. They would recognize their faces if they popped up amongst the stalls and shops. Alexandria's purpose lay in the fact that she would not be recognized herself. Upon a signal from the other heroes, it would be Alexandria who would engage the Warrior.

A foolproof plan, she thought. *Where no one knows anyone and everyone knows that.*

She turned her attention back to the monolithic monument in front of her: Rome's Pantheon. Inspired by Athena, or so Jasmin had informed her, and Olympus's temple complex, it stood as a testament to the grandeur of the past. Its front had the same bearings as the Parthenon in Athens, but behind it stood a square structure, and behind that peeked out the top of a massive dome. A triangle superimposed upon a square, superimposed upon a dome that burrowed itself into the ground behind the building, forming a chasm between the temple and the road. Everything about it was beautiful and majestic. Even the structures in Olympia itself barely competed, though Alexandria could not place her finger on the reason for that. Perhaps it was that this, however aided by gods, was made by mortals and therefore, its immortality was made all the more potent. Or perhaps it was simply that this grand structure was located in a narrow and assuming strait of Roman streets– a jewel tucked away into the everyday of the world Alexandria recognized.

She'd been confused when Jasmin suggested they begin in Italy and not in Greece; it had seemed strange to her. *But I guess it makes sense if Apollo believes she's here.* They had no other leads to begin upon, and the word of a god seemed as good as anything else.

"I think we're wasting our time."

Alexandria jumped at Jasmin's voice behind her. She craned her neck back and saw Triniya standing behind Jasmin, both of them smiling and decked in Italian flag-coloured scarves. "Oh?"

"If they're here, they're not coming out of the temple. We're better off going inside if you ask me."

Alexandria glanced at the crowds lining up to enter the

Pantheon and winced. “It’s going to close before we get to the front of that line.”

“We’re not getting in line,” Triniya rolled her eyes. “You couldn’t pay me to do that. There’s an entrance at the back of the dome... if you’re one of us. We used to use it as a resting place when we were on business in the mortal world. It was maintained by Athena’s Warriors before the destruction, but I don’t think it was ever really reopened afterwards. If they’re in the Pantheon, though, they’re using that entrance, I guarantee it.”

Alexandria stood up and stretched her arms over her head. “Well, then, I guess we better get the other two and go?”

Jasmin nodded. In tandem, the three of them made their way to the gelato shop. Alexandria’s sandals slapped on the uneven, rough cobblestone– it looked much older than anywhere she had ever been and yet just as sturdy and lasting.

“It’s strange to think that this used to be the epicenter of worship,” Jasmin nodded towards the Pantheon. “That was the temple to all the gods, not just a single one. Even Greece never compared in religious fervour to the Romans– the Romans were far more exacting and demanding of their faith than the Greeks.”

Alexandria hummed a chant she’d picked up from Priya and the Amazons during her free time as they walked, her feet landing with the beat.

“Find anything?” Wen-Tang asked once they were closer.

“We’re going to head inside,” Alexandria said. “If you don’t mind leaving your ice-cream behind.”

Wen-Tang scooped a large bite into her mouth, swallowed it, and then chucked the rest into the trash can. “Not at all. Back entrance, I assume?”

The three girls nodded. Brites frowned. “We might be walking straight into a lair of them. We’ll be caught off-guard and outnumbered if we do.”

"But we also can't waste all of our time sitting around here doing nothing," Triniya pointed out. "We're not actually on vacation, we're on a mission. We'll just have to be prepared going in."

Brites threw away the last of her gelato too and stared up at the Pantheon. Alexandria turned her gaze towards it as well. The sun was just below the horizon and the last of its orange glow was caught on the columns, casting the shadows of the Corinthian leaves onto the ground below. The church bells of the city rang all around, announcing the quarter of the hour, but not a single tourist dropped out of the line for the Pantheon, even though it closed in fifteen minutes. They could not bear to give up hope of seeing the inside. Alexandria admired their dedication, foolish though she thought it was.

"We best get a move on," she suggested. They all exchanged glances and nodded at one another. Falling into their positions– Jasmin at the head, Alexandria and Wen-Tang behind her, and then Brites and Triniya in the rear– they passed against the edge of the building. Alexandria craned her neck to look up at the roof, which seemed to stretch on interminably above her. They turned the corner to the back of the building and stopped. Jasmin peered down and pointed to a small incongruity in the stonework.

"Right there."

"How do we get down?" Alexandria asked. Instead of a response, Wen-Tang jumped into the chasm and land on a small platform that was nearly invisible from above. Alexandria grumbled and her eyebrows crinkled in annoyance. She never got explanations until way after the fact.

"Follow me!" the pirate exclaimed. One by one, the girls jumped into the chasm after her. Once they had all descended, Jasmin pressed against the stone, and it opened up into a passageway. They filed in and the further they went, the wider the tunnel became until it was as spacious as any of the temples in Olympia.

"The catacombs aren't the only massive underground structure in Rome," Brites told Alexandria. "Actually, we have networks like this around most of the Mediterranean. Back in the day, the followings rarely lived in Olympia itself– that was reserved for the gods and their children. We lived amongst the mortals, underneath their temples or in their forests and mountains– wherever we wouldn't be harassed easily. They knew we existed, of course, and often would provide us with food or shelter if we asked for it, but we stood apart from them because we had seen the gods and they had not."

"We lived here? But why? What did we do?" Alexandria asked. She tried to picture the Amazons spending an afternoon strolling around a Roman forum. There were no threats to the gods in the mortal world, no borders for the heroes to defend.

"The borders between here and Olympia used to be much thinner. Monsters would occasionally creep in, or satyrs and centaurs that needed to be herded back. There were far more demigods to protect or to shepherd to their parents when the time came."

"The world used to be more alive with faith," Jasmin interrupted, looking back from where she led the group to smile at Alexandria and Brites. "People used to believe in gods far more than they do now. Our presence among them was a kind of reward for it. Bring yourself closer to the heavens and they will come down to meet you. Once they stopped believing, we began returning to Olympia because there was no longer any need to protect them or serve them."

Brites resumed the story: "Ever since then, the mortal world's descended further and further into chaos. Take away faith and nothing will remain– not even vestiges of greatness. And the more time elapsed, the worse the mortal world became until Olympia sealed itself off almost entirely. Now, we very rarely enter the mortal world, unless we're collecting new followers. The fact that so many heroes are here at one time is anomalous. And the fact that Athena has founded her base of operations in the mortal world..."

"Is concerning," Alexandria nodded. "Got it."

The hall stretched on before them, but it passed quickly until they entered a large open space decorated with white columns and littered with sofas and stools, all seemingly untouched for decades. The piles of dust and eroded stone remained undisturbed on all of the furniture. No sign of the goddess they were searching for.

Alexandria wanted to meet Athena, if only to compare her to Ares. They were both war goddesses, but Alexandria was sure that they must differ widely in their approaches, if only by temperament. Nevertheless, Ares seemed to respect Athena and to hold her advice in high esteem– if what the goddess had told her before she departed for this mission was anything to go by.

"Should you manage a meeting with Athena," Ares had said. "Send her my greetings. Tell her that the owl's eye may roam wherever it so pleases, and it will always have the hawk's cry to accompany it."

"What is that supposed to mean?" Alexandria cocked her head. She had no time for riddles, not when the other heroes were waiting for her so that they could leave.

But Ares was almost jovial.

"The owl and the hawk have always stood by each other's sides, despite our disagreements," she said. "Athena is my sister-in-arms and I hers. In matters of peace, we hold the same council; in matters of war, we fight together."

"She didn't come running to your aid when you fought Artemis," Alexandria pointed out.

"She had only just returned. Her Warriors are far less bound

than most heroes: they come in and out of the group at will. Many of them leave to pursue education and enlightenment and return when they are ready. After the destruction, they simply dispersed back into the mortal world to pursue their own lives. Her plight was known to me and the demands of our sisterhood were relaxed for its sake. But there is nothing to hold me from aiding her now."

"I thought I was going to stop her. That was what the council decided. We don't know when Zeus will return, but we are certain that he will."

Ares scoffed. "The council may have decided one thing, but do not be so hasty in your judgement of Athena. She would make an excellent queen, far surpassing Zeus, and if the opportunity is given you to aid her... I expect you to uphold the desires of your goddess and to stick fast to her alliances, Alexandria. You may be a council member and owe some duty to your fellow heroes, but you are sworn in blood and flesh to me."

Alexandria scowled and crossed her arms. "I'll consider it," she decided, "and I'll pass your message along. Now, I've really got to go – I'm leaving Priya in charge."

"The Amazons have already been informed of the temporary change in command."

Alexandria nodded.

"Go with my blessing."

"I don't see any signs of life," Triniya said. She spun on her heel slowly, gazing around the entire space. "It looks, as you might expect, like it's been abandoned for several decades and we've just now stumbled in to disturb it."

"I agree," Wen-Tang said. She leaned down towards one of the couches and wiped a smear of dust off of it. Holding it to the lights, she shook her head. "It's the ceiling rock that's crumbled into dust. I guess without a goddess maintaining it, the halls are too unstable to last forever."

"Is it in danger of crumbling above us?" Brites asked, glancing haphazardly up at the ceiling above them.

"Probably," Wen-Tang shrugged. "But it doesn't seem that likely. When we get back to Olympia, though, I say we inform the other heroes that the Pantheon complex isn't a viable rest-place anymore until we fix it up. I'd hate to have an accident occur now that we've reopened the tunnels."

Jasmin crouched down to examine one of the other couches. "I don't recognize this furniture, though. Did anyone change it after the destruction? I was here right before then and we had the golden and white... but this looks grey to me."

"Are you sure it isn't the dust?" Wen-Tang asked.

"I'm sure."

"Guys, look at the ground..." Brites started.

Alexandria ignored her and looked around the room. Peering up into the darker corners of the ceiling, she startled. A pair of bright yellow and black eyes stared back at her. They blinked slowly. Alexandria stared at it. *The owl.*

"The hawk says hello," she mouthed, hoping that whatever strange owl was in the ceiling would understand her intent and forward it to Athena. Then, she turned to the group, her eyebrows still raised and startled, and said: "I think there's something in the rafters."

"You guys, there are footprints..." Brites started, still pointing at the floor, but everyone's heads snapped to the ceiling rafters at Alexandria's comment. The owl was still there, blinking slowly. It appeared completely unperturbed by the sudden attention. Slowly, it raised its wings and spread them out to their full span, tucked its chin into its feathery neck folds, and gave out one long *hoot* before taking off above them. The girls ducked. Its claws swung over them, missing them by a millimeter, but before they could even straighten up after the attack, Warriors of Athena poured out from the various hallways.

Alexandria and Wen-Tang pulled their swords out at the same time and met the charge head-on, whilst the others retrieved their various bows, swords, and knives. The clashes of steel and bronze echoed in the room, deafening in its timbre. Their shouts barely carried over the noise: everyone was screaming at each other, but no one heard anything.

Ducking to avoid a blow, Alexandria looked up at the grey eyes of the young man she was fighting. He was handsome, except for the thin lips that seemed to curl upon seeing her. It ruined his proportions and made him seem small and angry; made his eyes far too large for his head. He kneed her in the stomach and Alexandria went tumbling back.

"You-" she gasped, stumbling up onto her feet. She lunged at him, knocking him back against a column. He slipped to the side of it and pinned her against it instead.

She shoved against him just in time to tumble forward to the opposite side and avoid the strike. Falling into a somersault and landing back on her feet, she turned around to catch the guy again, but he had busied himself with Jasmin, his back turned away from her. Alexandria took a steadying breath and plunged her sword into his spine.

Everyone froze – the battle just simply *stopped*. Someone let out a cry of anguish and the Warriors of Athena all massed around the fallen boy. Alexandria stood to the side, her head slightly turned, staring at the blood on her sword. It was by no means the first person she had killed– many had fallen to her blade during the Hunter-Amazon war– but never had she seen a group huddle so quickly around their fallen warrior, stop fighting so quickly to protect the fallen body.

The girl who had cried out kneeled beside him, sobbing. She rested her head on his chest and grabbed onto his arms, her weapon cast to the side. Those surrounding her turned their gaze to Alexandria and her bloody sword.

They looked murderous and Alexandria unwillingly shrank

back. Before she could decide what to do, however, Wen-Tang swooped in in front of her, knocking back several of the Warriors. She grabbed Alexandria's hand and tugged her towards the exit.

"We've got to go– now!" she shouted.

Alexandria opened her mouth to ask about the others, but Wen-Tang answered before she had the chance to ask. "They're right behind us. *You're* the one that pissed them off!"

"I thought-"

"Later," Wen-Tang said, panting while she ran. She continued to pull Alexandria, her hand firmly grasping Alexandria's wrist so that it turned white, until they were standing outside of the Pantheon again. But she didn't stop there; she kept running until they turned into a small street and slowed to a walk. Wen-Tang led her into a tiny corner restaurant, and only then did the two sheath their weapons.

"Buongiorno," she said to the girl at the front, bypassing her without another word and pushing into the kitchen. The girl gave her a strange glance but continued with her work. Wen-Tang smiled.

"What are we doing?" Alexandria gasped, clutching at the stitch in her side.

Wen-Tang nodded to a cook, who shrugged his shoulders, looking very confused but too tired to deal with it, and continued on into a small room at the end of the kitchen. It opened into a staircase, which they descended until they were in a small apartment underneath the restaurant. "This restaurant is built on the foundations of an old temple of Apollo; it's not really a rest stop but I'm sure it'll serve us well enough for now. Jasmin will know to come here; she's probably heard about it from Apollo. He used to host parties here."

"What *happened* back there?"

"The Warriors take their dead very seriously." Wen-Tang shook her head. "Someone should have explained it to you earlier; there's no way you would've known. They swear blood oaths to avenge any of their fallen. They might not know your name or anything about you yet. But not only will they discover your deepest, darkest secrets now, they'll use them to kill you in some horrible and deadly way. If they get the chance."

Alexandria exhaled slowly. *Yeah,* she thought, *it would have been nice if someone had mentioned that a little earlier. Like, before I killed one of them.* "So, that's it? My life is on countdown now?"

"Not necessarily." Wen-Tang pursed her lips. "They might not have gotten a good enough look at your face to identify you– and there are ways to stay alive even if they have. You avoid them, you take extra precautions, you don't go on missions that might involve them..."

"It's too late for that. I can't just abandon you guys and go back to Olympia because I killed one of them."

Wen-Tang winked at her. "And then, of course, there's the solution I've been using for years now. You just never lose a fight to them. If you keep killing them, they won't manage to kill you."

Alexandria huffed. "I guess that's the only solution I have."

"For now." Wen-Tang motioned to the chair. "Sit down. It'll be a minute before the others arrive. They're going to have to stagger in so that we don't get noticed."

Just as she finished speaking, Brites strolled in. Dried blood crusted above her eyebrow, and she looked between the two girls with a tired, depleted gaze. "They're incredibly angry," she said. "We got out okay- the others are on their way. The Warriors will be on guard again now, though."

"Sorry," Alexandria muttered. "I didn't know we weren't supposed to kill them. I figured that was how skirmishes work."

Brites collapsed into a chair and rested her head in the palm of her hand. "It's not your fault. You're not in the wrong for trying to defend yourself. If we played by their rules, they'd be running Olympia, which is exactly what we're trying to avoid. We'll have to be careful, that's all. Or at least, unless we want to be seen."

Triniya and Jasmin came in at the same time, sporting matching cuts on their cheeks.

"It wasn't them," Triniya explained as she walked in, gesturing to her face. "We ran into a tree on our way here. I didn't see the stupid thing. I was so focused on making sure we weren't being followed and I dragged Jasmin right through it, too."

"That she did," Jasmin grumbled. "Is everyone okay? No big injuries?"

"We seem to have made it out fairly intact." Brites shook her head. "Thank the gods. We didn't learn much, but we know they have a significant force and that they've reopened the Pantheon underground– and I doubt that's the only rest stop. They've probably stationed people in several of our major rest stops. It's a safe and easy way to establish control of a city and it's no wonder the Olympians didn't notice it before; no one uses them anymore. They're basically defunct."

"So what do we do, now?" Alexandria asked, shifting from one foot to the other as the adrenaline in her body began wearing off. "We can't just go back to the Pantheon. We'll get attacked again."

"We were talking about it on the way over," Triniya nodded towards Jasmin. "Athena's probably at one of the rest stops and it isn't here–"

"What about the owl?" Alexandria interrupted, leaning forward.

"One of Athena's servants maybe, but not her. She would've come to the defense of her Warriors when she saw you kill one. But we've got to try and find her, and the best way to do that is to get a jump on checking the next location, before they send out messengers and warn the other rest-stops of us."

"That doesn't give us that long to get going," Wen-Tang pointed out. "Owls have probably already been dispatched."

"No," Jasmin agreed. "Nor does it tell us where we ought to go."

"That's easy," Brites said, and she pushed up from her chair. "We start where we should have started. We go to the Parthenon, in Athens."

CHAPTER 2
ATHENS, GREECE

Day 3

The soft glow of orange lanterns and white moonbeams lit the Parthenon with muted colours: its shadows were dark, harsh against the gentle light. A midnight sky stretched over the building, speckled with faintly glowing stars. The air was crisp and chilly, signs of an incoming storm from the coast, but at the moment, no clouds hovered in the sky.

The five girls huddled around their table just below the Parthenon, enjoying the last of their dessert. There was no reason to rush at this hour. The building was closing and soon, the last groups of tourists would descend the illuminated steps and retreat into the nightlife of Athens. Once it was deserted, they would clamber up themselves and the Parthenon would come alive once more with the same forces it had two thousand years before: the forces of the gods. Heroes would meet each other with their swords in a battle for dominance over Olympia and the mortal world.

Or, at least, that was the plan.

As she examined the Parthenon, Alexandria wondered if Athena really would camp in the most obvious place. She was a prideful, vain goddess, as they all were, and might certainly fall prey to the prestige of the Parthenon. Or her cunning and brilliance would win out and she would pick some smaller, lesser-known rest stop somewhere in the north of Europe. She couldn't tell. She was far more comfortable with Ares' rash whims than Athena's calculated decisions: they felt more intuitive, more natural. Everything Athena chose to do appeared to have several layers of planning and purpose to them. It made her nervous. She always felt several steps behind the goddess.

The lights dimmed on the Parthenon but did not turn off. It was closed and emptied; its small light show would remain for the rest of the night unless one of the heroes tampered with it to give them more cover in their sneaking and skulking. Brites stood up from the table and stretched her arms over her head.

"Well, I'm full," she said. "Going to head on a stroll. Anyone want to come?"

The other girls rose one by one, nodding in assent. Wen-Tang left a check on the table. They set off in pairs of two and three, exiting through the restaurant and onto the main street, rather than cutting through the small vineyard at the back of the patio and trekking through the grass. The soft lights of the street lit up their hair and cast shadows onto their faces; it made the whole place seem like it was burning embers or like there was lava running through the walls and down into the streets.

"You know," Triniya told Alexandria as they walked together behind the other three, "I haven't been here in centuries."

Alexandria raised an eyebrow. "How does time work in Olympia? No one ever explained that to me. You look like you're the same age as me, but you talk about being in the mortal world centuries ago. Keilee mentioned the same thing."

"Time flows differently in Olympia than it does here. I don't know what the exact calculations and ratios are. You're better off asking Apollo about that. Besides, the heroes of the gods have a certain longevity that only disappears when you renounce your position. It's all wonky and it shifts with the seasons and the solar positions, so it's not always exact, either. In the summer, days in Olympia might be weeks here and vice versa in the winter. Frankly, I've given up trying to figure it out and just say I'm eternally twenty, you know? There's no point in giving yourself a headache over it, that's for sure. It all evens out in the end, when we die."

Alexandria bit her lip and nodded. They wove in and out of streets, following Jasmin, Wen-Tang, and Brites' leads. "Right, so you were saying..."

"Mhmm, yeah– the last time I was here was several centuries ago, during the eruption of Pompeii. I had no idea about it at the time, of course, because that took place off the coast of Naples, but I remember hearing about it afterwards and thinking of the warm, sunny, delightful day I'd had there. My cousin died in that eruption, trying to rescue mortals. The lights just made me think of it. Funny how small things like that can spark memories that seem completely unrelated, isn't it?"

"I'm sorry."

"It's alright, it's been a long time," Triniya said. "I've come to terms with it. He was a Warrior of Athena, too."

"Not a Vestal Virgin?"

"Gods, no. He was a man. But families don't often serve the same gods, either. It makes it tricky when they go to war against each other. Back before the destruction, for example, the leader of Zeus' followers was a boy named Atar. He betrayed everyone, but his sister still serves under Wen-Tang and remains loyal to the Olympians. If those two ever crossed paths, I don't know what would happen. Loyalty to your god has to take precedence over loyalty to your family."

Alexandria frowned. She tried to imagine Carmen on the other side of a war between the gods. She imagined seeing her sister's face on the edge of her sword and attempted to picture stabbing or hurting her. Goosebumps rose on her arms at the idea. Her hairs stood on edge and her palms became sweaty. She didn't think she would be able to do it. Every muscle in her body seemed to freeze.

"That seems horrible," she finally said. Triniya's eyes were glazed over, and it didn't seem like she'd heard her at all. Alexandria gingerly shook her arm and Triniya snapped to attention.

"Sorry," she said. "Got lost in thought for a moment." She pointed towards the Parthenon. "Do you see that ridge of rock just beneath?"

Alexandria nodded.

"That's where our tunnel system is. It was its own complex, long before the Parthenon was actually built. Parts of it used to be above-ground– all before Athens was even a city. After Athena became the patroness of the new town, the complex turned over to her control and the Warriors became responsible for maintaining it– the same way the Oracles maintained Delphi and we Virgins maintained Naples. They decided to have the Athenians build the Parthenon on top of them. I'm not sure if the mortals knew about the complex at all, or only that it was already a sacred site so it made sense to build a temple over it. Regardless, they built the Parthenon following instructions inspired by Athena and she's protected the building ever since. It only got destroyed after the destruction– I wouldn't be surprised if slowly and almost imperceptibly, we start to see it come back into its full glory. Mortals won't even notice it's changed, really– they'll just assume it's always been in perfect condition. I've seen that happen before, a long, long time ago– when Rome burned down the first time."

"What do you mean?" Alexandria asked eagerly. There were still so many small things she didn't know about Olympia and about the history of the gods. She had no time to read or study its history, so she relied on the other heroes to tell her the most interesting facts they knew.

"Well," Triniya said, dropping her hand, "it was long before Nero and his fiddle, which is the story everyone remembers. An angry mob of Greeks set fire to the palaces and to the temple of Zeus. Once everything had died down and all that was left was ashes, Zeus repaired the whole city. It took him about a week, maybe, to do it the way he wanted, but in the end, Rome was returned to its former glory, and everyone forgot there was ever a fire. Not a single historical document mentions it– it's as if it never happened."

"How often does that happen?" Alexandria asked. "That events get erased from human memory?"

"Not much anymore." Triniya shrugged. They had arrived at the base of the Acropolis and Triniya paused at the foot of the steps, peering into the darkness above before she took a step forward and began the ascent. Alexandria kept right behind her, listening intently. "But it was common enough back in the golden age of Olympia. Gods were always creating messes that needed to be cleaned up, or humans caused disasters that we didn't want."

They fell silent, huffing under the exertion of climbing the worn, unused staircase. Jasmin, up ahead with the others, had led them to a side entrance, one away from all the security guards and checkpoints that would prevent them from entering unnoticed. Instead, they contended with broken pieces of rubble and long weeds scratching at their legs. Alexandria mulled over Triniya's words in her mind, breathing heavily. *How much of history is a lie? How much of it has simply disap-*

peared? She wondered if the Oracles had any archives that kept track of all these changes to the human world, or if it was a matter of having to have been there. *Have things been done in my lifetime?*

Blades of grass flashed in her mind, and she recalled the first moments she'd spent in Olympia, staring at that wide wondrous world, so confused and enchanted. Every blade of grass had been inscribed with stories, each vein of every leaf shaped to a human face, or the flames of a torch. The bark of the trees told stories, too, holding in their cracks and crevices tales of Olympia. Perhaps they contained within them the stories of the mortal world, too. Some oak deep in the Forest of the Dead was the guardian of the story of Rome's first fire. *I wonder if I could ever learn to read them.*

They reached the top of the hill. The Parthenon stood before them in all of its glory, tall, intimidating, awe-inspiring. The lights seemed to fade and all that was left was the soft moonlight casting its shadows in between the columns. The girls circled around and caught their breath, occasionally craning their eyes to see the top of the building or to marvel at the intricacies of the carvings.

"The closest entrance is in the middle of the ruins," Jasmin said. "We're going to have to be careful going in; we don't want to alert anyone to our presence until the last possible moment. We have the disadvantage so let's be smart: don't go off alone, stay in pairs, if we get outnumbered, scatter and meet at our safe spot. At the moment, we're not trying to capture Athena or rout the Warriors, we just want to know what they're doing. Until we do, we shouldn't engage unless we're attacked first."

"Doesn't it make more sense to capture Athena, bring her back to the gods, and let them deal with it?" Brites muttered.

Wen-Tang snorted. "Athena's impossible to catch. And as of right now, she hasn't done anything we can capture her for– as far as we know. Until there's proof, we have no grounds to stop her. That's why we're here– to get proof."

Brites cleared her throat. "Right, but Athena won't just give us information... are we supposed to sneak in on her telling the Warriors something?"

"It's not wise to count on that much good fortune," Jasmin said with a small smile. "Maps, materials, plans, drawings... anything like that would be a safe bet. Don't spend time trying to figure out what anything is, just grab and run. We'll decode it all once we get back– as quick as we can be, okay?"

"Then we should probably stop standing around here and get a move on. If anyone sees us, they'll raise an alarm, and we won't even know it."

Wen-Tang slipped a knife out of her pocket and nodded. Leading the way, she stalked to the middle of the Parthenon. Just as she kneeled down in order to loosen the stone that opened the entrance, a blood-curdling howl exploded. It shook the foundations of the columns and deafened the girls.

Alexandria crouched down instantly, her skin tingling with fear and anticipation. Her hand moved to her side, and she rested her palm on the hilt of her sword, scanning the horizon for any sign of an incoming force. Vaguely, she was aware of the presence of the other girls: Wen-Tang had abandoned the stone and now hid behind a column, her knife glinting in the moonlight, and Brites, Triniya, and Jasmin were huddled together in a mass of fallen stones. Alexandria could only hear her own breathing now, feel the palpations of her heart. They seemed to push against her leather amour, as if her heart was trying to exit her chest. She lifted her hand off of her sword and pressed it against her chest, trying to rein in the terror. There was no time to be afraid of whatever had made that noise.

Slowly, she crept towards Wen-Tang, staying low to the ground. As she passed over the center stone towards the column, another blood-curdling scream arose. She launched herself towards Wen-Tang and pressed her back against the pirate's. The heat of a familiar body calmed her nerves slightly, but her eyes darted back and forth.

"Something's here," she whispered.

"Be ready," Wen-Tang ordered. She pressed her lips together into a tight line and scanned the top of the Parthenon, looking for any signs of movement. Alexandria watched Wen-Tang pale, and she remembered their conversation earlier. *Wen-Tang is also being hunted.* "They know we are here."

Alexandria glanced at the center stone, expecting at any moment that it would unleash a horde of Warriors who would kill them all within an instant. But the stone did not budge and no earthquake underneath them suggested life. The whole world seemed deathly still, deathly silent. There was no wind. Only the pounding in her chest told her it was not a dream. Alexandria lifted her eyes to the moon. Its light seemed to have faded, overcome by the shadows. It sent another shiver down her spine when it disappeared completely behind the clouds. Even the human lights shining on the Parthenon could do nothing to pierce the deep veil of darkness that had overtaken the place.

Alexandria's breath hitched, caught in her throat. The beat of a wing filled her ear, sounded like a deafening drum. Still, there was nothing to see. The moon came back into view, but it was a grey speck, no longer bright and white. The wings returned, flashing in front of it. And once more, the ghoulish scream reverberated in their ears. The foundations of the Parthenon shook at the sound.

The anticipation of the moment was shattered with a horrendous explosion of movement as three monstrous creatures descended from the sky and attacked.

"Furies!" she heard Jasmin cry out. But the words seemed of little importance to her. What did it matter who these creatures were? They were attacking. The only important thing at the moment was to return the attack with equal vigour, to survive. As she was backed into a corner, a weight settled in Alexandria's chest. Nothing would be simple about this quest in the mortal world, nothing at all.

She slashed at the Fury and its talons brought her back to reality. Chaos surrounded her, yet Alexandria faced her Fury alone. The monster scratched at her cheek, and blood ran down onto her neck. She retaliated by slamming her sword against its leg. The Fury faltered back. Alexandria pounced in front of it, bringing the hilt of her sword down on its head. It collapsed onto the ground and did not rise again.

Brites and Triniya teamed up against one of the Furies. Jasmin and Wen-Tang fought against the other one, working seamlessly with each other to keep it too distracted to land any hits. Together, they easily brought it down and high-fived each other over their win.

Breathing heavily, Alexandria traced the outlines of her deep cut with her finger. She pulled it away to look at the bright red blood as it trickled down her finger and dripped onto the ground. There were the tiniest specks of gold in the blood now, a consequence of being a hero of Olympia. She wiped the rest of the blood on her pants, squeezing her sword underneath her arm, and then tore a piece of her tunic off to hold up to her scratch. It didn't seem to be too bad, but there was no telling when they would be somewhere she could take proper care of it. *It is better safe than sorry,* Alexandria thought. She rejoined the others, still holding the faux gauze to her face. They were all congratulating each other, patting each other on the back, and commenting on how easy the Furies had been to defeat.

"They work for Athena now?" Alexandria interrupted. The weight in her chest sparked with rage at seeing them so engrossed in meaningless matters. There was work to do and they were still in a vulnerable and open position. Immediately, the other heroes sobered, though whether at her question or her tone, Alexandria wasn't sure.

"They wouldn't have attacked us otherwise," Jasmin said. "Unless we committed a grave blood sin, which we haven't, as far as I'm aware."

"No," Triniya agreed. "Athena has somehow managed to recruit them to her side. Perhaps that ought not be surprising. They are creatures of justice and after Zeus, Athena is the most just of the gods."

"We should either leave or go in," Alexandria said through gritted teeth. "Standing here talking is a waste of time. We can debrief later."

"We came all this way." Wen-Tang nodded in approval. "What more do we have to lose?"

She pulled open the stone and this time, no sounds released– the tension in Alexandria's shoulders relaxed slightly and the tight feeling in her chest subsided. Sheathing her sword, she jumped down the hole after Wen-Tang and was shortly followed by the other girls. They found themselves in a well-lit and spacious set of hallways, clearly built purposefully and not tunneled into a pre-existing location like the Pantheon. She matched her pace with that of Wen-Tang but neither of them spoke as they tread down the corridor. At the halfway point, there was a tall oak door that stretched from the top to the bottom. A doorknob gleamed in the light of the torches in the hall, and intricately carved mythological scenes in the wood beckoned for their attention. Alexandria paused to stare at the door, wondering what stories it depicted– were they forgotten ones, like that which Triniya had told her?

"I don't remember that being there," Jasmin said, coming up behind her. "Open it."

Alexandria dropped her gaze from the carvings and pressed the palm of her hand on the doorknob. It yielded to her touch and the door swung open to reveal a massive library swallowed in bright lights that seemed to emanate from the books themselves. The shelves formed a semi-circle around a large, mahogany desk covered in maps and papers, so thick and spread out that were it not for the wooden legs, it would be impossible to tell what kind of structure was holding them up. Persian carpets lined the floors in bright reds and subdued blues.

"It's beautiful," Jasmin said, running her hand across the spines of a nearby shelf. She bent her head to look at the titles. "I don't think the Oracle libraries have most of these titles..."

"Don't get distracted," Triniya clucked her tongue. "We don't have time to go book-shopping. Those papers look promising, though."

"This is far too easy," Brites scowled. "There's no way they've left all of this ripe for the picking."

"We can deal with that later." Jasmin shrugged. "When else are we going to get an opportunity like this?"

"I'm just saying, I think we should be careful," Brites retorted.

Alexandria agreed with her. It was stupid to think that the Warriors had simply forgotten these papers. Either they were meant as a diversion and held false information, or there was some kind of trap. But she did not voice her opinion.

Jasmin and Wen-Tang had already begun rifling through the papers: picking them up, examining them closely, shooting cursory glances over other ones, shoving them into their pockets. Alexandria stayed at the edge of the room, observing the proceedings. It felt like a foreign scene to her, a mission she was intruding upon and not something she was a part of. She looked up at the tops of the bookshelves and once again, her eyes met yellow rounds. The owl was back, perched in the single dark corner of the room, staring down at her and the other girls. She could almost imagine the smirk of distaste on its beak. Blinking, she watched as, somehow, its beak formed legible words:

The owl greets the hawk.

Glancing around quickly, she realized that no one else had heard the owl speak. They were all still preoccupied with their rummaging. Her gaze shot back to the ceiling, wondering if the owl would say anything else to her, but by the time she found the dark spot again, the yellow and brown had disappeared once more. Only shadows remained.

Alexandria leaned against the doorframe and crossed her arms. She had no idea what she was to do: betray the strange alliance between Athena and Ares, or betray the council of Heroes, or simply go behind both of their backs and attempt to resolve the conflict herself. *Things were almost easier when the biggest pain was handling Keilee and Priya*, she thought.

Then, out loud, she said, “We shouldn’t linger any longer than we have to. Brites is right about this being suspicious.”

Wen-Tang crammed one last handful of papers into her back pocket and dusted her hands off. “I think we’ve gotten everything useful out of this place without doing a deep search. Jasmin, Triniya, you ready to go as well?”

Jasmin clasped a small book to her chest and nodded. “But I’m taking this, if that’s all right? I’ve been wanting to read it forever but there are no copies left in Olympia or anywhere else I can find.”

“When are you going to find time to read?” Brites raised an eyebrow. As Jasmin tucked the small book into her overfilled pocket, she shrugged and hummed something noncommittal. Triniya simply laughed.

Alexandria exited the room without waiting for them to follow. She stared down the corridor, hand on her sword hilt, waiting for a contingent of Warriors to appear, but none did. They left the tunnels and replaced the stone on the Parthenon floor without any incident. The moon had returned to its bright, clear glow and danced along the edges of the marble as they descended the steps back into the wild underbrush and the uneven stairs. The walk was silent the entire way back. A weight seemed to have descended on all of the heroes, though Alexandria couldn't figure out why. But leaving the halls had felt difficult and dreary, and the gentle, cool breeze blowing on her face did nothing to alleviate the feeling.

They entered the town but no longer were there any glows cast on the buildings from streetlights. They had all been extinguished by wind or human hands, and darkness surrounded them. Slowly, they felt their way to the inn they had booked rooms at. The front desk was deserted, not a soul to be seen.

Climbing up the stairs, they wished each other good night in mechanical voices and decided to look over the strange papers in the morning, over cups of coffee. It was too late to decipher anything was the consensus, and nothing could be done with any new information at this hour. It made perfect sense to wait.

Without surveying her room at all, nor even stripping down completely– she took off her weaponry and armour and left everything else– Alexandria collapsed onto her bed and immediately fell into a heavy sleep.

Interlude
An Inn in Athens

Day 3

The pressing weight did not leave her; it felt like the world was tilting, waiting expectantly for a large break in reality. The tension grew, eating away at Alexandria's body... and then it disappeared.

The release was almost euphoric when she was swallowed whole by the ground and spat out on a strange, inconsistent, indescribable plain of colours and sensations. The wind was deafening and swirled her hair around her face, blinding her. Alexandria reached out with her hands, looking for something to stabilize her. The ground shook beneath her. Voices screamed above her. It was all a haze, reminiscent in a way of that red dreamscape where she had met Ares, but at the same time, entirely different. It felt cold and empty. There was nothing for her hands to grab onto. Everything seemed to swirl in a state of half-being around her.

"What's happening?" she tried to shout, but the words were

carried away by the wind. She couldn't even tell if she'd succeeded in making any noise.

Alexandria, be careful.

She recognized the intonations and in a weak breath, she uttered: "Chaos."

It is I. Olympia continues to teeter on the edge of the survival. Zeus is returning to Olympia and with him, he will bring the power of the throne and the godly council back. Beware of interference from more than just Athena and her heroes. There are other forces at work that I do not control.

"What do you mean? Do you always have to speak in riddles? What's happening that you aren't controlling?"

There are not riddles, but hints to the greater story. You are not privy to the same information that I am, mortal, and if I told you things as I saw them, your mind would be unable to grasp them. It is better for you to grasp small bits of it that will guide your actions.

"Then do you have any idea what I should do about Athena?"

You have sworn allegiances, Alexandria, and you must hold to them, whatever they cost you. Olympia and the world are held together by oaths sworn and kept, and to destroy them is the gravest ill you could commit. Remember your oaths.

Alexandria woke with a start, falling onto the hard, uneven, wooden ground with a thud. Her throat constricted with panic and fear, but she was unable to scream or groan. The visceral recollections of the dream haunted her. She could still feel the wind blowing in her hair and the desperation to find something to hold onto. Her heart battered against her chest. The minutes felt interminable. Chaos had never been this haunting or felt this dangerous; last night was a fever dream of worry and pain.

"What the hell..." she finally whispered to herself. She stood up and looked out the window of her room. The sun was beginning to peek over the horizon and the courtyard in front of the hotel was awash with pinks and oranges. The fountain sputtered and splashed with birds. Everything was peaceful, as if the nightmare had never occurred. Alexandria found that to be the worst of all.

Jasmin was seated on the edge of the fountain, her hand outstretched. Alexandria wondered where she'd found crumbs to feed the birds with, but they came to her willingly, pecking at her fingers and landing on her shoulders. It seemed like a scene too peaceful for the horrors of the night or the gravity of their quest. The colors of the sky glowed in Jasmin's hair and on her tunic, which had once been cream but now resembled more of a patchy grey from all the dirt and scuffing.

Alexandria fastened her belt on and tied her cloak; it was still chilly enough in the mornings to need it. She attached her sword to her belt and stepped outside of the room. *Lucky that mortals don't seem to notice the swords,* she thought to herself as she did. *They're completely oblivious.*

The hallway was deserted, but the lights were on, and the smell of fresh pastries wafted from the dining room. They did not entice her. She entered the room– it was also empty– and secured a cup of coffee. Nursing it in her hands, Alexandria walked into the courtyard and settled herself on a bench a few feet away from Jasmin. They did not speak to each other; there was nothing to say. The others were still asleep at this early hour and any talk of strategy and tactics would wait for the proper morning time.

Breakfast time finally arrived. Jasmin pulled her feet up to the edge of the chair and tucked her chin on her knees, holding a cup of tea in front of her. She watched silently as the other girls piled their plates of pastries and fruits onto the table and settled down. Wen-Tang and Jasmin pulled the papers out of her pockets and placed them in the center. The small, hardwood surface was engulfed by the large stacks. Jasmin reached for one of them and gently uncrumpled it. The handwriting along the edges was illegible and blotched, but there was a map in the middle.

"This is a map of Greece," Jasmin said. "We're here, in Athens." She pointed to the star on the map and leaned over to show Wen-Tang.

"What's the other star?" Wen-Tang asked.

Jasmin tilted the map to the side and then straightened it in front of her. She placed her coffee mug on one edge, resting it on the compass. "It's the temple at Delphi, I think. There isn't really anything else in that direction."

"There's another underground rest stop there," Brites piped in from across the table. "Probably barely functional, but we used it in our time." Jasmin nodded.

"The Oracles maintained it, but we abandoned it long before the destruction because no one needed the oracles anymore. It's too far away from any major city to be useful." The sunlight fell through the window onto the map, dancing in their coffee cups and sparkling on the dewy fruit on their plates. Without the swords and grimy clothes, it would almost have been beautiful.

"But there's a lot of power there," Triniya said. "There's an opening to the underworld in the cave."

"Well this map is labelled Delphi," Alexandria said, pulling out another one from the pile. "It looks like schematics of the building."

"There's a star over the underworld cave," Wen-Tang said, pointing to the dot on Alexandria's map. "If we knew what the stars meant, we could probably figure out what Athena was planning."

"What if these are all fake plans that we were meant to find?" Brites suggested. "They were incredibly easy to steal, and no one tried to stop us. If we head to Delphi, we might be heading straight into an ambush."

"This map has the Pantheon starred, too, though," Triniya said. "So far, they've all seemed to correspond with places that Athena has been or has repurposed. There's no reason to believe that Delphi isn't another one."

"So we would absolutely be walking into a trap if we went," Brites sighed. "But if we want to catch Athena, we might have to."

"I guess we head to Delphi, then." Wen-Tang rifled through the rest of the papers. "All of the rest of these are scraps of the Odyssey and the Iliad translated into different languages, I think."

"We can leave for Delphi after I finish my coffee," Triniya agreed, leaning back in her seat and picking up her mug. "But I'm not leaving before I do."

CHAPTER 3
THE TEMPLE OF DELPHI, GREECE

Day 5

O*nce upon a time, the temple must have been overwhelming,* Alexandria thought. Her cheeks felt warm from the climb up the side of the mountain. Delphi was strangely accessible, though her feet still ached from the rough rocks, but her spirits felt high for the first time since the Parthenon. For whatever reason, despite the fact that hiking or walking had never been a great joy of hers, the trek to the temple had been truly joyful. She remembered all of the days she'd spent with Carmen in the mountains and even the pang of desire for her sister could not dampen her spirits. The sun felt warm and shone bright, and the ruins of Delphi were beautiful. The chattering between Triniya and Jasmin behind her was irrelevant small talk: they had already decided all of the details of their entry on the road to the mountain.

They didn't stand around and enjoy the elegiac beauty of the ruins. Alexandria unsheathed her sword and Wen-Tang stepped forward to loosen the stones and open the entrance. Efficiently and with deathly silence, they entered the underground chambers. They did not halt to look at the friezes on the walls or appreciate the ornate golden decorations that the Oracles had placed everywhere long ago.

Alexandria looked from side to side and let her eyes pass carefully over the small, dark corners as they walked by them, wondering if the owl would be here. It seemed to be following her to every location, after all.

"That's where the entrance to the Underworld is." Wen-Tang pointed to a small side chamber. It was pitch-black and eerie in comparison to the rest of the tunnels which were bright and somehow airy. Alexandria poked her head in and then immediately retracted it, waving at the girls to be quiet.

"There's something moving in there, I think," she whispered.

"Hmm?" Wen-Tang turned around and backtracked a couple steps to stand next to Alexandria. "Where?"

Alexandria carefully pointed at what appeared to be a shadow roaming around the edges of the room.

"What is that..." Wen-Tang trailed off, squinting to try and see better.

The shadow jumped out at her and all the girls fell back to the other side of the hallway, knocked off their feet with varying yelps and shouts. Dazed, they stood up one by one, grasping for weaponry to counter the attack.

"Do not pull out your swords on me," a voice thundered. All of them immediately dropped their jaws in fear and surprise.

In front of them was a tall, menacing figure with eyes so dark the irises couldn't be told apart from the pupils: they were just black masses surrounded by stark white. The man himself was ghostly pale and gaunt, with long fingernails and a ragged black beard. His long hair curled down his back and an ivory crown rested atop his head, jagged and rough, as if it were meant to resemble a set of shark teeth. The clasps holding his white chlamys to his black robes were in the shape of skulls. The only piece of colour on his entire body was the ring on his finger, which was crimson and gold wound together. It appeared like a star against a dark night.

Everyone gasped; the air seemed to still. The god towered in front of them. The recognition sunk in. *No one knew he was here,* Alexandria realized. Her skin prickled with a chill, her breathing was shallow and cold.

Once the shock finally dissipated, Brites was the first to drop onto one knee, and the others followed suit. "Lord Hades," she said. Alexandria cast a glance upwards.

So this is what Hades looks like, she thought. It wasn't at all how she'd imagined him. In her mind, he had been far bulkier, more like Poseidon. There seemed to be no family resemblance whatsoever. *His eyes are terrifying.* He reeked of death and decay, and it made her shudder. She was glad she did not serve Hades as... a ghost, or whatever his heroes were. Ares was a far more amenable goddess to be attached to.

"Brites. How interesting to see you– and your companions– out in the mortal world, let alone the unused rest stops. Might I ask why you all are here and not in Olympia?"

"We've been sent on a quest," Brites said. "We believe that Athena is attempting to make a bid for throne, and we have been sent to stop her, or to at least discover what her true machinations are."

"And Artemis could spare you?" He did not ask about Sophia. Alexandria assumed it was because he knew; she would be in the underworld now. "None of your gods sent their second-in-command?"

"No," Jasmin answered. "We decided this quest was important enough for our presence. Athena is a wily goddess and difficult to pin down. This is the third place we've tried to find her."

"She is not here," Hades rumbled. "I am sorry to inform you. I would know if my niece was roaming halls I have claimed as my own for the present time."

Alexandria swallowed hard. That sounded an awful lot like a threat– they were trespassing into Hades' territory, and he didn't seem like the kind who would easily forgive them for the transgression. She stilled her breathing, preparing herself for an inevitable conflict.

"Our apologies, Lord Hades," Brites said smoothly. "The information we retrieved from the Parthenon suggested we would find her here. We had no intention of intruding; we did not know that you had claimed the Delphic temples as your own."

Hades hummed. "I will forgive you this trespass, this one time, for the sake of my friendship with Artemis. And for the sake of keeping Athena away from the throne of Olympia, I will even do my best to provide you with some guidance. Recently, a Warrior of Athena ended up in the Underworld. Perhaps it would be enlightening to speak to it?"

Alexandria blushed, a prickle of unease in her stomach. The man she'd killed. She exchanged glances with Brites quickly. The other girl seemed just as nervous to take the favour as she felt.

"Come now, there's no reason to be worried," Hades chided. "Ghosts and ghouls are under my control. It will not harm you, nor will it speak unless it is answering a question posed to it. It is entirely safe, so long as I am here with you."

There's no way we can politely refuse, Alexandria thought. Brites must have had the same idea because she bowed her head again and said: "Thank you for your generous offer, Lord Hades. We accept."

"Excellent!" He clapped his hands together. "If you will step with me into this room, ghosts cannot wander too far from Underworld openings, even when under my jurisdiction."

Silently, and with paled faces, they filed into the room one by one and formed a semi-circle around the opening to the Underworld. What little light there had been seemed to disappear and the only thing left glimmering was Hades' ring, the crimson and gold seemingly emanating their own glow. The light spread across Hades' body and face so that he seemed to be enclosed within a golden halo.

Hades closed his dark pupils and began to chant words that Alexandria didn't recognize, in a language that seemed older than even time itself. It reverberated in her bones and though she did not know the words, she understood the meaning. He was calling on Death to temporarily release a soul from its torturous chambers and to let them enter the light for a brief moment, that he may consult them. She found it fascinating that Hades seemed to be deferring to a greater, darker, more ancient power than himself and that he had not simply snapped his fingers and made the Warrior appear.

Slowly, from the bottom of the opening arose a pale blue specter, with gashes across its face. It was clothed in a simple tunic and bore no other ornamentation, save for the bracelet around its arm with the owl pendant, denoting it as a servant of Athena. Despite its haggard and grotesque appearance, it was unmistakably the boy that Alexandria had killed in the Pantheon. Her stomach curled. She'd never come face to face with someone she had killed before. This was how she would look once she finally lost to someone else's blade. The idea was nauseating.

"Ask it whatever you desire," Hades said, dark eyes flicking open again, "that might aid you in your quest." He stepped to the side to allow the girls to crowd around the ghoul as closely as they felt comfortable. But none of them moved, too horrifyingly entranced by the sight.

Alexandria was the first to break from the grasp of terror.

"What's your name?" she asked it, the words coming unprompted from her lips.

"Albert," the ghost said in a flat, monotone voice. There was no animation in his face. His jaw seemed to have not moved at all, his lips barely parted. The dull scratchiness of his tone irritated Alexandria. Wen-Tang pressed a hand to her back.

"Albert. How long have you been serving Athena?"

"A year."

"When did she recruit you?" Wen-Tang persisted. It dawned on Alexandria that the ghost, though compelled to provide the information requested, did not want to and would only give out the barest of details. He was somehow still loyal to his goddess, even in death.

"When she returned from Chaos."

"So she's been operating in the mortal world for a year," Alexandria said. "Is that correct?"

"Yes." The answer seemed pained, as if the ghost had tried his best not to utter it but it had been forced out of him.

"Where is Athena now?" Jasmin asked.

Albert scowled, biting his lip. But another force pried it open, and the words came tumbling out of his mouth, "Alexandria."

Everyone's heads spun to face Alexandria, who frowned and shook her head. "I don't know where Athena is," she said hastily. *It's not as if I've been carrying a message from my goddess to her this entire time. There's no way Albert knows about that.*

"Alexandria?" Brites repeated, slowly averting her gaze from Alexandria.

At this, Albert clearly couldn't resist. For the first time since he appeared, he seemed to actually desire to speak. "The library in Egypt, you idiot. Why on earth would I mean your silly companion? Where else would Athena deign to build her fortress but the center of all knowledge and learning of the gods?"

"Alright, alright," Wen-Tang snapped. "We get the point. Tell us about Athena's plans for taking over Olympia."

"I was not privy to them," Albert said. "I did not hold a high enough rank to be given sensitive information."

"Is there anything else we should know about Alexandria before we go find Athena there?" Jasmin asked.

A devilish grin appeared on Albert's face, matched, Alexandria noticed, with a devilish grin on Hades' face. A feeling of dread crept upon her and before she had the chance to say a word, the doors to the room slammed shut and Hades' ring darkened. The room fell pitch-black, except for Albert's wiry and pale form. The girls drew their weapons again, realizing they had been caught and as they did, they heard Hades laughing at them. But he'd disappeared: only his disembodied voice remained.

"For the sake of my friendship with Artemis, I granted you an audience with a ghost. But I have an alliance with Athena that I must honour. You all must pay with your lives. Still, one of you may return to Olympia, mute and scarred, so that the gods know what happens to those who try their hand against the Lord of the Dead and the Owl. No longer will I sit in the shadows of Zeus and his children– I will take my rightful place as the eldest son of the gods! And as for the one who will survive, Athena has granted that mercy to you, Alexandria, to thank you for the aid Ares has promised her. Though it is unlikely you will continue to serve as Ares' hero, I would imagine, you will see the fruition of your promises to Athena. You are, even now. She has decided to let you live."

"What did you do?" Wen-Tang shouted at her.

"I didn't do anything!" Alexandria screamed. Albert lunged at her and his ghostly hands felt slimy as they pushed her against the wall.

"Don't be modest, Alexandria," he taunted. "You've been speaking to Athena this entire time."

"I've never seen her!" Alexandria protested as she pushed him off of her and fell to the ground. Other ghosts began to pour out of the opening to the Underworld and soon, all of the heroes were occupied with fending them off.

Albert chased Alexandria vindictively. "The owl you have seen is Lady Athena. All owls are her servants but only she has eyes of that colour."

"Tons of owls have yellow eyes," Alexandria wheezed, strained from fighting the slippery ghosts. "There's nothing special about them."

"Yes, but did you see black pupils in that owl's eyes? You fool. It is in the uncanny details that one finds the hints of the divine. Athena has no pupils as an owl; she has no need for them because she does not see in the same way that humans do. You should have known. Fool."

Alexandria tried to swing a knife at the ghost, but it passed through him. He didn't even show a scratch. Alexandria backed away from the irate ghost and found herself back-to-back with Jasmin. "We can't beat ghosts- we can't kill them."

"I know," Jasmin rasped. Alexandria managed to glance back at her; her forehead was scraped and bleeding and there was a wild look in her eyes. "There's no way to get out of this room."

"They'll kill us! And if they don't, we'll just starve to death stuck in here."

She felt Jasmin become deathly still behind her and then she felt her hand grasping her shoulder. "We have to jump."

"What?" Alexandria blurted out. "You want us to jump into the Underworld to escape the ghosts that live in the Underworld? That makes no sense!"

"You're not the one they're trying to kill!"

"I can explain-"

"Save it for later. There are tons of entrances and exits from the Underworld. We just jump in and we'll find an exit to somewhere else. We'll blend in among all the dead– these ghosts won't be able to find us and even if they could, they won't be animated. They'll return to their docile state."

"How do you know?"

"I read it in a book once!"

"But Hades is the one who made a deal with Athena; he wants to kill us."

"Do you have a better idea?"

"No-" Alexandria started.

Jasmin grabbed her hand. "Then we jump!" she shouted for the benefit of the other girls. Trusting they had heard, she pulled Alexandria into the hole, and they went tumbling down into the dark, dark netherworld.

CHAPTER 4
THESSALONIKI, GREECE

Day 5

Josephine dipped her toes into the cool water, gazing out at the sea. It was just on the edge of the sunrise and the sun hadn't quite peeked out from behind the ocean yet, but the sky was already glowing with strips of pink and yellow, slowly coming to life from its dull, dark blue. The beach scuttled with activity as crabs scurried to and fro from their small burrows, poking their heads out of their sandy homes to greet the new day. Not far from the shoreline, a pack of dolphins leaped from the water at random intervals. If she looked closely, Josephine could see the small fish in their mouths as they jumped: breakfast time at this early hour. Tucking her chin into her knees, she closed her eyes for the briefest moment and then opened them to look at the sky once more. Her book and pen lay by her side, untouched, as she took in the sights of the early dawn.

It was the only time to herself she ever had, the precious hour of uninterrupted solitude which she found so crucial to her sanity. Once the day began for all of the Warriors, it was always mayhem and madness and frantic running back and forth with updating plans and new communications, trying to keep track of all the various outposts they were establishing in the mortal world as strongholds from which to take Olympia. She could look forward to being bombarded from all directions with requests, demands, and pleas, once she returned. Not that she would complain, naturally. Josephine adored her role as Athena's hero. It was all that she had ever wanted. The constant streams of new knowledge from the books she found tucked in every corner of Athena's libraries, the mastery of combat she had always craved as a young martial artist, the sense of control and purpose she felt in her role...

Blowing her pale curls to the side, Josephine picked up the book she was reading and flipped to the correct page, playing with the pen in her free hand. Every so often, she would bite the cap off and scribble something in the margins or underline a sentence. Several pages deep into her new novel, she was interrupted by the arrival of a handsome young man, with wind-blown hair and bright grey eyes. *James.* Her heart fluttered with excitement, and her cheeks flushed red. He was the best part of her time in Thessaloniki.

His searching eyes were the mark of all of Athena's heroes. Taking on Athena's blessing and protection changed their eyes into the same grey as the goddess. Josephine found them exceedingly attractive.

"Is it time already?" she said, her mouth forming a pout.

James shrugged. "We could always start operations without you, but I have the suspicion that would make things far more difficult and disastrous than if you came back to the real world."

Josephine looked out at the sea for a brief moment and nodded, standing up with her book and pen in hand. "You're right. There isn't a moment to waste, especially with how close we are."

They began walking back together, James' hand resting on the small of Josephine's back to help her through the rocky terrain back to the temple. "An owl from Athena arrived today informing us that the Olympian heroes fell for our dupe of the Delphi temple. That should be the last we hear of them. Hades won't fail in his job to kill them, I'm sure."

"Let's not celebrate prematurely," Josephine replied. "I've heard rumours of those girls from the older Warriors. They're tenacious– they survived the destruction and the upheaval afterwards. That Wen-Tang is especially notorious. We have a death pledge against her, and she's managed to evade our grasp for decades at this point."

"That's not possible," James frowned.

"It's not *supposed* to be," Josephine corrected him. They arrived at the edge of the temple space– above ground, it only looked like small piles of rocks and clumps of wildflowers and weeds– and Josephine knelt down in the center of it to trace her finger along the pattern hidden in the stone, opening a wide hole beside her. She and her companion hurried inside. "Which is why it's so formidable that she's managed it. Maybe we've gotten her at last through Hades, but we won't be sure until his missive arrives. Until then, we ought to assume they're still alive."

"Well," James continued, "that's only part of what's come in overnight. The Warriors in Alexandria have scuffled with some priestesses of the Egyptian gods."

"You're kidding," Josephine groaned. "What are we supposed to do about that?"

They strolled down the hallways, watching as it went from empty to packed with Warriors rushing back and forth, some holding missives or massive maps. Josephine contemplated with some degree of amusement as a few of them, on their day off from the hustle and bustle of military life, carried piles of books to their rooms to lock themselves away and read. Piles of books far larger than one could get through in a day.

"Tell them to route them from the library, I guess. I doubt the Egyptian gods will try and challenge Athena's right to the library. Frankly, it's the least of our problems at the moment. The London Warriors have reclaimed the tunnels under Midras' temple and want to know if they should expand. They mentioned wanting to push further north into Scotland and Ireland. The Olympian heroes caused havoc in Rome, and the Warriors there need us to make that death pledge against Ares' hero. Got the message earlier."

"We already did that."

"Not everyone; just the council and the Warriors stationed here. We need to pass along the owl to the rest of the Warriors around the world."

"We can do that later today; is there anything pressing or strategic we need to deal with?"

"Yes." James opened the door to the council room. "We need to decide where we will push into Olympia from and when we want to launch our initial attacks."

"What are our latest updates from Olympia? Have our informants given us anything since two days ago?" Josephine asked. With a smirk, James pulled a roll off the table in the middle of the room.

"It came in this morning."

Josephine hurriedly unrolled the parchment and spread it on the table, leaning over to read it. At first glance, it appeared to be mostly jargon: dates and names and numbers and abbreviates dotted a rough map of Olympia. But Josephine wasn't yet interested in that portion of the message. She skimmed it, her eyes dropping to the bottom of the page, where their informant in Olympia had added his own notes and observations.

War is threatening to break out in Olympia. The North Guard has begun to press its luck with the Amazon fortress. Zeus has finally returned and reclaimed the throne of the gods– our sources indicate that Poseidon and Artemis have taken offense to this and are only reluctantly following him. They may be persuaded to back Athena should they be approached carefully. Our sources also inform us that Ares appears to be fully backing Zeus. We are not yet sure if this is a ruse or if Ares has broken her agreement with Athena. Further updates as information accumulates. Due to location constraints, we have not yet confirmed if Aphrodite has returned but there were disturbances at her temple. Further updates as information accumulates.

Zeus' new hero is named Cernhelm and he has taken control of the Amazon forces, with the Amazon Priya serving as his second in command. Expected unison of Olympia forces against the threat from the North Guard. It is expected that there will be much friction and inter-fighting as the war comes to a head.

Josephine flipped the scroll to read the other side of it.

The leader of the North Guard has been confirmed as still being Atar, the previous head of the Sons of Justice. He is not yet dead. He is operating with an unconfirmed second in command, but all sources suggest that it is Keilee, previously an Amazon of Ares. Further updates as information accumulates.

Suggested course: do not attack whilst Olympia deals with the North Guard. Slow down all operations until this war has ended. Olympia will be at its strongest while combatting the North Guard, as all forces will have united and will be on guard. It is recommended that the attack is prepared and ready to launch at any time so that the invasion can begin as soon as the North Guard is defeated and peace appears to have settled in Olympia. Their guard will be at the lowest at this time, during the celebrations, and the council will just have disbanded and disarmed. Further suggestions in next missive as information accumulates.

"Well?" James asked as Josephine raised her head and

rolled the scroll back up. "What's the news? Anything we didn't know already?"

"A lot," Josephine said. "Olympia's in the middle of a war with the North Guard."

"That makes it the perfect time to strike them!" James exclaimed. "They'll be distracted and their forces divided."

"No." Shaking her head, Josephine tossed the scroll into the chest of old missives they kept on the edge of the room. "The informant has suggested we wait until this war has cooled down and the Olympian Alliance has dissolved. I agree with him. They move slowly and once they've disbanded, it will take them time to reunite again– by then, we'll likely already have won. Besides, the North Guard might do some serious damage to their numbers, making the job easier for us later– and at less cost of our own lives. We ought to let the Guard do the hard work for us."

"What if it drags on?" James asked with a frown. "Athena is patient, but that won't last forever."

Josephine snorted and nodded her head towards the door. With an understanding look, James stepped back two paces and closed it. Sure that no one would come in on them, Josephine continued: "No gods are patient, but what Athena wants is to win the throne. She'll understand if we must delay our operations in order to ensure the best possible chance of success. She's a strategist; she'll understand where we're coming from on the matter, I'm sure. Besides, I'll be the one to deliver the news to her. You need not be concerned about any outcome."

"You telling Lady Athena we'll be postponing operations is precisely what I'm afraid of," James muttered, crossing his arms. "You may be her hero but that doesn't necessarily protect you from her whims of rage."

"You're being dramatic." Josephine rolled her eyes, taking a step closer to him. "She's the one who told us to be careful in the first place."

James stepped forward as well, wrapping his arm around Josephine's waist. "Forgive me for being worried," he said. "I cannot help it, with everything progressing the way it is. It seems like at every turn, we are being thwarted."

"Is this about me or Olympia?" Josephine whispered, tucking her head underneath his chin and leaning against his chest. "Do you miss it?"

"Of course I miss home," James murmured. "But there's nothing stopping me from going back if I wanted." Then, he scoffed, "As if I know where home is anymore. It's you I'm worried about more than anything. This was supposed to be an easy, simple coup against Artemis and maybe Poseidon, and now we're contending with almost all of the other gods in this weird power vacuum. It feels far more dangerous than it did two months ago. Let alone a year ago, when we started planning it."

A great commotion began to stir outside the door. From its small window, Josephine could see people running back and forth with renewed vigour. James heard it all and pressed her closer to him, dropping a soft kiss onto her head. "I think our goddess has just arrived for the morning council," he said.

"I'm of the same opinion," Josephine laughed. "Shall we go out to meet her?" She pulled away from him and proffered her arm. He took it with a small bow.

"We shall indeed, Josephine."

He opened the door, and they joined the bustle heading to the entrance to greet Athena and prepare for the strategic meeting of the day.

CHAPTER 5
THE UNDERWORLD

Day 5

They huddled against a pile of rocks, hidden in the shadows, watching with faint worry as the ghosts circled around the entrance several times, waiting for movement. The hole in the sky above them loomed: but the ghosts did not follow after them. A fissure in the darkness of the oppressive landscape, it seemed to beckon the heroes, filling them with hope. But the ghosts stayed, until one by one they dissipated, as if they were being called back to their homes. The heroes did not breathe a sigh of relief until they had all dispersed back into their various habitations in the Underworld. Alexandria stood up, stretching her legs out. She turned to face the others, and her breath caught in her throat.

They no longer looked like themselves. They had faded into pale blues and greys, straddling the line between living and dead. In panic, she looked down at her own hands and noticed that they, too, were blue. She closed her fists and felt her nails dig into the palms of her hand. Relief flooded her veins. She only appeared dead. She was still solid and living and she could feel her heart pounding in her chest.

Triniya laughed nervously, her eyes darting back and forth. "It's weird."

Alexandria raised an eyebrow at her, lowering her hands again but keeping her fists closed. The digging feeling in her skin was comforting in this strange and new world.

"When you enter the Underworld," Triniya explained, "you fade to half-ghost, that's what all the scrolls say. You can't die unless you're killed, but the Underworld sucks some of the living out of you. So we look like ghosts and the longer we spend in here, the less solid we'll become– but we are still alive. It's just an odd sensation; nothing to actually worry about yet. I think. I hope. I don't know."

"It's unsettling." Wen-Tang frowned. "I'm not a fan either, Alexandria. I say the faster we can get out of here, the better. The ghosts might not be able to touch us but we're in Hades' home territory now and apparently he wants to kill us."

"Then why isn't he here?" Alexandria asked. "This is his territory; couldn't he just appear and kill us right now?"

"He can also wait us out until we give up. It's far more economical when you have hundreds of minions at your command to do the work for you... if we don't get out of the Underworld, he's won. And there's only a limited number of entrances and exits, most of which are guarded."

"This one was the one Orpheus used," Jasmin nodded. "That's how Triniya and I knew it existed. Fortunately, it's the least guarded, because it's mostly been forgotten. We might get lucky."

"He'll manage to kill us," Triniya groaned. "That exit right there is our only shot."

"Well, kill everyone except Alexandria," Brites reminded

everyone. Alexandria gave her a look. Of all the things that was important right now, this was the least of them.

Jasmin frowned. "What did he mean by that, Alexandria?"

Alexandria shrugged. "I'm not sure. I haven't done anything to jeopardize the mission, I promise."

Wen-Tang took a step forward. "Are you sure? If you've done something, it's better out with it now so we can fix it."

"There's nothing to fix," Alexandria protested.

Slowly, deliberately, so that Alexandria could watch it happen, Wen-Tang placed her fingers around the hilt of her knife and pulled it out, letting it rest against her thigh. "What did you do? Why does Athena want to spare your life? What makes you so special to her?"

Alexandria rested her hand on the hilt of her own sword and cocked her head. "All I did was pass on a message from Lady Ares, as my goddess requested of me. I didn't give her any information, and I didn't betray any of you– if Athena wants to keep me alive, it's as a service to Ares."

"They have always been close," Triniya muttered. "I don't think we can blame Alexandria for Ares and Athena being chummy."

"Maybe not," Brites said. "But we *can* blame her for speaking to Athena and not telling us she was. How often?"

"Twice," Alexandria replied cooly. "The owl."

"Athena was there, and you didn't tell us?! That's our whole mission!" Wen-Tang exclaimed. She lunged at Alexandria with her knife and Alexandria pulled out her sword and swung it at the other girl, knocking the weapon out of Wen-Tang's hand. Enraged, Wen-Tang spun back at her and pulled out her own sword. They clashed once more, and the sound of steel echoed around them. Neither of the two girls heard the shouting from the other girls telling them to stop. Nor did they stop– Wen-Tang sliced Alexandria's shoulder and Alexandria grazed Wen-

Tang's leg– until Jasmin and Brites grabbed onto them and pulled them apart by force.

"Drop your weapons!" Jasmin screamed.

Brites wrestled with Wen-Tang and finally secured her sword, holding it away. "Calm down," she ordered. "Killing each other doesn't solve any of our issues!"

"She betrayed us!"

"I did what I had to do!" Alexandria snapped. Jasmin held her back.

"We'll come back to this later," Brites announced, daring either of the girls to defy them. "But right now, we need to get out of the Underworld before Hades finds us. So put a pin in it and let's find an exit to the mortal world again."

With a scowl, Wen-Tang pulled away from Brites' grasp and glared at Alexandria. "Fine. I'll deal with the Amazon later."

Alexandria felt a pang in her chest as Jasmin released her. The pitiful smile that Triniya gave her did nothing to alleviate the sense of dread in her bones. That heaviness in her stomach returned, and her chest seized with fear. Had she ruined the council of heroes beyond repair so soon after its foundation? Would she become ostracized from the only peers that she had in Olympia?

Her eyes blurred and she had to force herself to refocus. There was no time to feel sorry for herself. She squashed the feelings down as best she could and shoved her sword back into her sheath.

"Later," she agreed in a terse voice. "How do we know what direction we should go?"

"We have no way of knowing," Triniya said. "We should just start walking and keep our eyes peeled for any ghosts. It's a straight shot to that exit over there... I think. I can't actually tell."

"Sounds like the best plan we've got," Jasmin shrugged. She adjusted the sleeves of her tunic and began walking in the exit's direction without waiting for any of the others to join her. It was the one shaft of light in the place, a clear, gleaming goal to march towards. The tall, spiral staircase reaching from the ground to the top of the shaft of light taunted them with every step. They exchanged looks– except for Wen-Tang who refused to look at Alexandria– and trailed after the Oracle of Delphi. Alexandria lingered behind all of the others, watching as they formed their small groups and began chatting on their walk. She relished the silence and the chance to think on her own. About what she needed to do about Ares and the other heroes.

How is it so hard? she wondered. *If Athena is trying to pull us apart so she'll have an easier time taking over Olympia, it's working.* She'd never seen Wen-Tang as angry as in those few moments prior; if she'd expected anyone to be angry about her secrecy, it would have been Brites. It was Brites who'd been harmed the most by the machinations of Amazons before– Keilee had killed Sophia, after all. And Brites was the one who'd brought the whole thing up to the heroes instead of letting the matter lie.

The silence was deafening as they walked across the barren wasteland of the Underworld. There was a steep decline to their right that resembled a riverbank that had entirely died. The red earth was scorched and charred– Alexandria could see the black stains of a wildfire that must have spread through. If there had been water at one point, there was no more. Everything was dry and dead. The sky, if it could properly be termed a sky and not just the underbelly of the earth exposed, was black and desolate. With all its various hanging root systems and dark humus occasionally giving way under the weight of all it carried above it and crashing into the ground of the Underworld, it formed craters. Certainly, there were no stars or anything resembling it. All the light of the place seemed to emanate from the not-river, which cast an eerie orange glow.

Alexandria strayed from the back of the pack for a few

minutes to walk along the edge of the bank and discovered that it was indeed a river: a river of fire. Huge, massive flames tunneled deep, deep into the abyss, launching out on occasion up from the darkness. *Like solar flares.* Alexandria watched in awe at the majesty of the flames dancing in the river. She didn't notice the other girls draw further and further away into the horizons until they were but little specks. All of distance and proportion seemed skewed and broken below the earth. What felt like minutes later, she finally looked away from the mesmerizing sight and found herself alone.

Crap, she thought, panic beginning to rise in her chest again. She had no way to navigate this strange land on her own; if the other girls were to be believed, there was no actual way to navigate it at all. She'd lost sight of the small stream of light that demarcated the exit point, and the chance of finding it again seemed low. Let alone finding the other heroes. Alexandria clenched her fists and forced herself to breathe. She could figure this out. She was the heroine of Ares and not a powerless mortal. All she had to do was find the exit out of the Underworld and then reunite with the other heroes once she was back in the mortal realms.

"Probably best to follow the river," she mumbled under her breath. With a determined step and eyes averted from the majesty of the river of fire, she marched on. Time stretched on and her feet grew sore; the silence began to weigh on her. Triniya was not useful for much, Alexandria didn't think, but she was a good companion when you wanted someone to talk your ear off. As it was, she now only had her thoughts to keep her company.

It seemed unlikely that Wen-Tang would forgive her any time soon and Alexandria didn't believe Brites would either. She doubted Jasmin or Triniya would care enough to hold a grudge. But there was nothing she could, or would, do to make up with Wen-Tang and Brites. She was not about to grovel at their feet for simply trying to play the role of an Amazon Queen. She owed them no explanation for her decisions. They could take it up with Ares and Athena; Alexandria was simply the middleman between gods. What could a mortal do against that?

"Whatever," she told herself, kicking a loose red stone into the river. The fire roared around it. There was no point in dwelling on the squabble with the other heroes. The far more pressing matter was Hades' alliance with Athena. If Athena had managed to secure the allegiance of the eldest god and that of the war goddess, she posed a genuine threat to the throne of Olympia. Not for the first time, Alexandria wondered why Ares had allowed her to go on the mission if she had a pact with Athena. "Not my job to wonder about," she said out loud, trying to convince herself.

She was just doing what she needed to, to keep her goddess happy and honour her council of heroes. *Politics are hard.* Keilee had been good at it, playing each side for what she needed from them and all the while having her own plans. If she'd had the chance, Alexandria could have learned a lot from Keilee, who'd survived the destruction and become the bane of the Olympian council. That took a political ability and conniving spirit that Alexandria worried she didn't possess. This quest seemed to be exposing all of her inadequacies.

"Alexandria! There you are!"

Alexandria's head shot up and she saw Triniya waving at her. All of the heroes waited a few paces ahead. Wen-Tang's arms were crossed and she gave Alexandria an annoyed stare as she got closer. Triniya seemed entirely unphased and Jasmin and Brites were deep in conversation and didn't pay her any mind.

"Got distracted by the Phlegethon?" Triniya asked. "It's impressive. It looks like what I imagine a solar flare would look like– just not as hot."

Alexandria nodded. "It's definitely that," she said. *Leave it to Triniya to do her best to pretend that nothing has occurred to rift the group in two.*

"I've only been here once," Triniya continued, wrapping an arm around Alexandria and leading her onward. "It must have been back in the heydays of Olympia because I was a new hero of Hestia and not very old. Most of our acolytes start out very young, you know– not quite children, but not as old as Ares recruits her Amazons. Hestia took us on a tour of all the kingdoms of the gods. Hades was the worst of the lot, for sure."

Alexandria hummed. After the sharp silence of her solitary walk, Triniya's overwhelming chatter was somewhat comforting. In a strange sense, it felt like being by a fireplace and listening to a rambling story over mulled cider and warm pastries.

"Don't worry about Wen-Tang," Triniya continued. "We hammered it into her that she can't just attack you like that. We'll need to hear you out, obviously, on any interactions you've had with Athena, but I trust you, Alexandria. I know you wouldn't do anything to jeopardize the mission or the council. You're not like Keilee."

What if I wanted to be more like her?

Triniya interrupted herself when she spotted the Underworld exit they'd been walking toward: the tall, spiraling staircase that led up to an open wound in the sky-ground, flooding its local area with the brilliant, dazzling brightness of sunlight. Alexandria imagined the warm feeling on her skin and found that she missed it already.

"How long have we been in the Underworld?" she asked Triniya, who simply shrugged in response.

"Hell if I know. Time in the Underworld works even more bizarrely than in Olympia. But come on, we're almost there!"

INTERLUDE
THE COAST OF THESSALONIKI

Day 5

"Your informants are wise."

"Thank you, Lady Athena," Josephine inclined her head slightly, but the gesture went unnoticed by the goddess walking beside her. "So you agree that we should wait for the North Guard to finish fighting Olympian forces before we strike."

"I do." Athena pursed her lips and stopped walking. She stared out at the sea for several long seconds, the air punctuated with the sounds of waves crashing into the rocky shore. "I know the leader of the North Guard– he was long before your time, Josephine, but trust me when I say that he was a formidable warrior. His name was Atar."

"My informant mentioned that in his missive. People don't seem to like him," Josephine said. "Why?"

"He was Zeus' hero, the leader of the Sons of Justice.

Beloved by all, adored by the Olympian council. Even Ares, who likes so few people, appreciated his company. In the heydays of Olympia, he was engaged to Ares' heroine, Penthesilea, and then broke it off when he fell in love with a Huntress named Jari. But no one ever faulted him for that. They all liked him too much. That, of course, all changed on the day of the gods' destruction."

Even the sea seemed to darken at those horrible words. A shudder ran down Josephine's spine and she closed her eyes briefly. So many horrible stories had been shared with her about those terrible days. Though she had not even been born, she felt as if she had stood there and seen it all happen, so vivid were some of the memories imparted by older Warriors.

"He led the charge to defeat our enemies whilst we gods met in Olympus to think of a plan to stop the betrayal of our children once and for all. But when we arrived on the battlefield, Atar inexplicably turned on us. He began to kill the gods one by one. The first to fall was Dionysus– and then Hermes. Ares and I fell fighting side by side and that is all I remember. I can only assume he completed whatever devilish plan he had because the gods are only now returning to Olympia, after who knows how long spent in the void.

"No one knows why Atar betrayed us the way he did; nor, I suspect, does anyone care. All that matters is the simple act of betrayal. I would assume, though this is merely deduction and not something I actually witnessed, that upon ending the battle, Atar left Olympia, knowing he would no longer be welcome among its lands.

"The North Guard seems to be his collection of the rejected from Olympia: mercenaries, betrayers of the gods, assassins. If Atar alone was able to destroy the gods, I have no doubt his small band of traitors would be able to seriously damage Olympia."

"It's a smart plan."

"There is a common saying among mortals, that the enemy of one's enemy is one's friend." Athena nodded. "I have always found it to be a particularly useful nugget of wisdom, and I wish I'd come up with it myself."

"Did you not?"

"Contrary to what some might believe, not every wise thing originates in me. A great deal comes from Apollo, which is why the prophecy scrolls in Delphi have proven so useful in our calculations. Have you had the chance to look them over?"

Josephine nodded. She'd stayed up late for several days in order to do just that: pouring over scroll after scroll, trying to decipher the puzzling rhymes and discern if they would be useful for their purposes.

"There was one that particularly stuck out to me," she said. "The only one from the Sybil of Cumae."

"Mhmm," Athena hummed. "I recall that one with great clarity. It also made an impression upon me. *Go forth amongst the ruins of the old and conquer lands of which once it was told, that peace and stability were easily found. Where now however is chaos and distress. A land long ago lost to destruction, conquer, conquer, the olden lands, and place a new crown upon a new throne.*"

"The notes in your archives said that prophecy referred to the Roman conquering of Carthage," Josephine said. "Which seems to fulfill it very well– but it also does seem to fit perfectly with Olympia. A land lost to destruction? That would be the destruction of Olympia that's come to pass, wouldn't it?"

"So I have been led to assume," Athena replied. "The difficult thing about prophecies is that often enough, they apply to more than one occurrence. It is therefore hard to know when it has been completed once and for all and when it has not."

"I thought they were for individual times?" Josephine scrunched her face. "What's the use of a prophecy if it keeps repeating?"

Athena shook her head. "Mortals never discovered that secret, so we kept giving them prophecies. But all of history simply repeats; it is but a cyclical calendar of events stretched over centuries. There is an inception, a rise, and a fall– and so again, a new inception. The Greeks were followed by the Romans, followed by the Europeans, now followed by the Americans. The advent of unbelief and forgetting about the gods has, in a sense, led to a fracturing of the cycle, since one of the primary duties of the gods is to maintain this calendar. But without believers to worry about, we have become so disinterested in the mortal world that we have allowed it to blow off its course. There ought to have been a fall several decades ago, and there was not. Now, it has been so long that I am unsure of what it would take for it to be fixed."

"You'll fix it when you become queen of Olympia, then?"

"Indeed. For the gods are also able to remove events from the annals of history. From time immemorial, we have controlled the flow of history. I intend to resume that role once I am queen."

Josephine felt her stomach turn slightly at the idea. She had, of course, heard from other Warriors about the influence the gods held over the world and how little mortals were aware of it. She had read scrolls that gave her doubts and made her suspicious about what really happened to the heroes the gods used for their own gain. But to hear Athena declare her plans to control the mortal world so stringently scared her. There was something deeply unsettling about power and such overt displays of it.

She opened her mouth to press Athena further on her plans when the ground beneath them began to shake, and a small hole in the sand, rumbling and growing larger, swallowed land into it. It groaned like it was loath to give up its treasures. The very air seemed to vibrate with the sounds of the earth.

The waters of the beach receded. Out poured figures, ghostly and pale, with indiscernible faces.

Josephine reached for her sword when all of hell broke loose.

CHAPTER 6
THE EXIT OF THE UNDERWORLD, GREECE

Day 5

Just as they arrived at the exit of the Underworld, it seemed like the entirety of hell stirred with rage. Hades' voice rose above the clamour of hundreds of ghosts pouring from every direction to surround the heroes.

"You thought you could leave my lair alive? Athena will not be the one to claim victory over you if I have any say in the matter."

The voice rumbled through the earth, shaking the ground. Alexandria stumbled against her own feet; Triniya caught her arm, manipulating her so that they stood back-to-back. In tandem, they nodded toward the other. Their weapons shimmered in the harsh light of the exit. Alexandria exchanged looks with Triniya, and her eyes roamed the other girls. There was clear determination in their eyes, all of them: they knew the goal. To attempt to cut a path and run. As soon as they were out of the Underworld, they would be safe from Hades' vindictive spirit.

"Of course, I had to wait until you were so close to safety... that will make my victory all the sweeter, won't it?" Hades continued. "Seeing the end of the danger– and yet not managing to reach it. But how convenient it is that you're already in the Underworld! You'll be processed immediately into your final destinations– unfortunately, I fear the judges will likely assign you all to Elysium for heroics. If I could, I would override their decisions."

Venom dripped in his voice, genuine outrage that he could not control their afterlives. *What had Athena promised him that made him so vitriolic? Or is this just always the way he is? Desperate for death?*

Still, she knew, the anger of a god was something she was equipped to handle. She was a trained fighter, the hero of Ares. As Queen of the Amazons, the anger of her opponents worked in her favour. They made mistakes in their rage, and she could spot them easily, since Ares was the goddess of anger. Alexandria scanned the surrounding ghosts quickly, looking for the way to the exit.

There seemed to be no way to push forward without fighting, but that worried her since their weapons had seemed ineffective against the ghosts during their last skirmish. And then, it dawned upon her. It wasn't foolproof; they would still need to hold their own against the ghosts, but it gave them a better chance at winning against the hordes.

"Triniya!"

"Got a plan?" Triniya asked. "Any time now would be good if anyone had any thoughts..."

"Turn into a sparrow," Alexandria said hurriedly. "And fly to the exit. Once you're on the staircase, turn back into a human. We'll keep the ghosts busy until then, but then I bet they'll try and chase you– and we'll get swept along to the exit with them."

"That seems like a terrible idea," Wen-Tang scowled. "Too many things could go wrong."

"Do you have a better idea?" Triniya asked.

"What if they don't follow you? You'll be isolated– we wouldn't be able to help you if they attacked-"

"I'll just climb up the stairs," Triniya shrugged. "And we're running out of time– they're going to overrun us any second!"

"Ok, ok!" Wen-Tang snapped. "We'll do Alexandria's idea!"

Without further ado, Triniya disappeared in a poof of feathers, reappearing as a tiny, flitting sparrow. She flew over the horde of ghosts and the other heroes quickly lost sight of her as she became just a tiny speck in the vast expanse of darkness.

The ghosts overwhelmed them and soon they were far too busy evading the deathly grips of the cold, slippery ghost hands, somehow both material and non-material at the same time. Alexandria plunged her sword into one of them and pulled it out. Just like in the chamber at Delphi, her blade didn't harm the ghosts. All it did was keep them at bay. They still feared weapons, even though they wouldn't harm them. But Alexandria's arms were weary; she sheathed her sword and grappled with the ghosts instead.

Like when I used to fight with Carmen over stupid things, she thought. *But now it's for my life against a bunch of deadly ghosts.* Sometimes, Alexandria grabbed onto to what felt like real flesh; other times her hands passed right through the phantoms. They seemed to shift between solid and ghostly with no rhyme or reason. *They're haywire.* She fell to the ground as she wrestled; around her, the other girls came to the same realization and also abandoned their weapons in exchange for their fists. It was a very temporary solution to their issue, but the ghosts were too weak to pin them down as long as they kept thrashing around.

Alexandria's arms grew heavy and tired. It felt like the fighting had been stretching on for half an hour, even though she knew it could only have been a couple of minutes. Her foot sagged for a brief moment and a ghost latched onto it with vigor. She barely managed to shake it off.

"Over here!" Triniya shouted from the staircase. In unison, the ghosts looked up from their current victims and, en masse, frantically marched towards Triniya at the exit. *They are so simple-minded*, Alexandria observed wearily. *But that doesn't mean we can defeat them easily*. As tired as she was, she forced herself to stand up and chase after the ghosts, jostling through them to get to the staircase. She could feel the presence of the others around her, doing the same thing, just as exhausted. But they pushed through the exhaustion– they had to. It was a matter of survival, not choice.

The group of them reached the staircase with the first wave of the ghosts. Alexandria's feet weighed heavily as she forced herself up the stairs. Her calves burned from the fast-paced climb. Triniya grabbed her hand and dragged her higher. They burst onto a beach, sparkling and dazzling with light, thinking they were safe.

Alexandria was ready to collapse onto the sand. Every bone in her body was sore and weak. She felt as if she'd been thrashing and fighting for hours, though she knew it had only been a matter of minutes. The adrenaline in her body began to ebb as the feeling of safety settled on her. Her eyes burned under the bright sun as they adjusted from the darkness of the Underworld. She tried to catch her breath, but just as her knees promised to buckle, she saw the tell-tale grey eyes of a Warrior. Looking up, she realized it was not simply a Warrior.

It was Athena. Confusion clouded her face, framed against the ocean and the sky. She seemed surprised to see the heroes pop out of the ground; the girl next to her seemed equally shocked. As if they'd be caught unawares mid-conversations. But then that look faded... and Athena appeared furious.

She seemed to move faster than sound as she launched herself upon Alexandria before the other girl had the chance to hear her cry: "Hades, you useless buffoon!" Alexandria swung to the side and pulled out her sword again. Her limbs screamed and she felt unable to hold the weight of her weapon.

Parrying a blow from Athena, she angled herself so that she could watch as the other heroes, all exhausted, crawled out of the Underworld. It was not simply that they had exerted themselves, Alexandria realized as she watched colour return to Jasmin's face– they had been in the Underworld so long they had taken on more attributes of ghostliness than mere appearance. They had become sluggish and slow, just like shades. The longer she parried blows, unable to land one on Athena herself, the more energy Alexandria felt returning to her bones.

Jasmin and Triniya fought as one unit, moving in and out of sync, against the other young woman that Alexandria didn't recognize or care about– the girl was nothing compared to the goddess she was desperately trying to stave off.

The beach shifted with her steps, and her feet sunk into the soft sands. Athena used it to her advantage, forcing her to stumble back into the waves, throwing her even more off-kilter. The cold water smashed against her with a distracting irregularity. Brites emerged from the Underworld and joined Triniya and Jasmin– Alexandria lost sight of them and their battle when Athena stepped forward, filling her whole view. *This is the end,* Alexandria thought, *it's all over from here.*

Athena raised her sword to strike, Alexandria to block– but the strike never came. Wen-Tang leaped onto Athena's back and tried to slip her knife around her neck and press it against her throat, but Athena kept moving back and forth, throwing the pirate off-balance. All of Wen-Tang's efforts were focused on finding the chink in Athena's armor that would let her land a hit and disable the goddess for a brief moment.

Finally, Wen-Tang succeeded in her goal and caught the goddess' throat with the edge of the knife. Athena flipped her off her back and rounded upon her, absolute fury in her eyes. A small trickle of golden blood fell from her neck down into the folds of her chlamys, staining the soft grey.

"You will pay for that, you insolent whelp!"

She brought down her sword upon Wen-Tang, but just as the blade fell, Alexandria flung her body over the pirate's. The blow landed upon her chlamys and bounced back, and Athena stared down at the girl, comprehension dawning on her face.

"You're Ares' hero. I had not noticed your aura," she breathed. "I cannot harm you because of our pact. Step aside and let me kill Poseidon's insolent twit, and I will let you live."

Alexandria shook her head. "I'm not moving."

Athena pushed her boot against Alexandria's stomach. "I can't kill you, but I can harm you if you stand against me. Do not make that mistake, girl– I bear no ill will against you just yet."

"Over here!" Jasmin, Triniya, and Brites shouted in unison. Athena turned her head towards the sound, giving Alexandria a chance to stand and pull Wen-Tang further away and drag her to her feet.

The other three heroes, while Alexandria and Wen-Tang had been occupied with Athena, had disarmed and tied the Warrior up. They now held her in front of them, dangled like a prize before her goddess. Her wide eyes looked between her goddess and the other two heroes, but she did not speak.

"Tell us what your plan is," Brites demanded, "or I'll kill her." She gestured to their prisoner with her xiphos.

"Never." Athena took a menacing step forward. Brites' arm hovered closer to the captive's neck, the tip of the blade now resting on the skin. The goddess' eyes seemed to glow for a brief moment before they faded back into the cool grey they usually were.

"I'll do it, I swear I will. Why do you want to take over Olympia?"

"You cannot be that naive." Athena stepped forward again. "Do not pretend you are not interested in what I do. Olympia has fallen into disarray under the leadership of Artemis and Poseidon. It must be corrected, and I am the only goddess strong enough to do so."

"What about Zeus?" Jasmin exclaimed. "The king of the gods will take his throne back as he should!"

"Zeus's control has been waning for centuries now. He is far past his prime; it is time the country passes to the next ruler. Me. We used to rule the mortal world and now mortals have forgotten about us entirely. I will reclaim our right to it, just as I will reclaim my right to Olympia."

"You know we won't let you," Wen-Tang hissed from the other side. "We'll stop you, whatever it takes."

"Perhaps you might have." Athena smiled. "But your people are at war right now and they will be weak– they will gladly bend the knee to a power that will protect them."

"What do you mean by that?" Alexandria gritted her teeth. She found it hard to believe anything that Athena said– it all seemed true, yet so easily contrived by a goddess of wisdom. And she was still shaken from the blow that her cloak had blocked. *How had it done that? And why?*

"That is not information I will give you," Athena said. "And you are running out of time, heroes. I have summoned the other Warriors to me, and they will be here very soon. Hand over my hero, now."

When did she do that? Alexandria wondered. *She's got to be lying. We've been fighting her the entire time.*

"No," Brites replied evenly. "We'll let her go if you swear on Olympus that we will walk out unharmed and undisturbed."

"Never!" Athena shouted. She seemed to grow in stature and, suddenly, towered above all of the heroes, who had to crane their necks to see her. "You will not bargain with me! Hand over my hero!"

Brites pressed the blade to the prisoner's neck hard enough for a tiny rivulet of blood to appear. "If I press any harder, she will die."

"Then so be it," Athena announced. "A life sacrificed for the goals of her goddess! That is a noble way to die, my hero." And she launched herself at the group of girls. But just as she reached them, Hades appeared from the Underworld and threw himself at Athena.

"How dare you interfere with my prey!" He threw a punch at her face and landed it. "You promised I could end them! I should be the one to take their lives!"

"They will be yours!" Athena howled. "As soon as they are dead! Stand aside!"

"I was promised the chance to have them alive– I need servants in the Underworld, now that I have no following! I was going to use them! They can only serve them if I kill them!"

"You can find other mortals!"

"I want the heroes of the other gods! So I can lord it over them for all time!"

Taking advantage of the momentary distraction, the girls began to run, dragging Athena's hero behind them as a possible hostage– or informant, since Athena had seemed less than preoccupied with whether her hero lived or died. When she briefly looked back to observe her, Alexandria could tell that the news had shaken the girl: she seemed pale and worn, and not simply from the small injury inflicted by Brites or the battering endured from Jasmin. She seemed scared.

Well, Alexandria thought, *you should be.*

CHAPTER 7
KAVALA, GREECE

Day 5

"You must be new." Jasmin stared down at the girl in front of her. "What's your name?"

They hadn't bothered tying her to anything: she seemed far too defeated to attempt an escape. And she was smart, she must be, since Athena chose her; she knew she could not outrun all of the heroes.

Of course, that did not mean she was not reticent. It was the third time Jasmin had asked the question and Alexandria was beginning to lose her patience with the whole endeavor. Everyone was tired and cross now, and a headache throbbed in the back of Alexandria's skull.

She leaned against the windowsill and turned her head to look outwards at the city beneath them. She could see the mountains of Delphi on the horizon line. *What a strange town.* She'd never heard of Kavala. Never had the name of this bizarre and wonderful city crossed her path, but Alexandria was glad they'd chosen to lay low here for a while. Every house on the street seemed to be painted a different color, making the whole thing look like a parade of gaiety. There were red houses with yellow accents, orange ones with blue, even a bright teal one with a dark red roof. As she watched people move up and down the sidewalks and motorcars pass in the road, she pondered the Warrior's reticence. *It's annoying. I don't have time for this. We need to wrap this mission up. Someone get her to talk.*

"Why do you care so much about your silence?" Jasmin asked Athena's hero, sharply. "Your goddess was willing to sacrifice your life for her goals. Do you really still owe her your allegiance?"

The reminder of what had transpired only a few hours earlier seemed to startle the Warrior. She glared at Jasmin, her mouth setting into a hard line. "Lady Athena had a greater plan, I'm sure of it. She would not have offered me to die unless it was the only possible path to success, and in that case, I would gladly have laid down my life."

"You're insane," Alexandria snapped, her lip curling. *This is going to drag on forever.*

"I am a Warrior of Athena."

The room, hollow and empty, echoed their voices. It was almost devoid of any furniture beyond the bare necessities: tables, chairs, beds. Most of it was old and creaky, but heavy. The walls were bare. Curtains flapped in the wind, hitting Alexandria's back as she turned to watch the scene before her.

"Her hero, we know," Jasmin continued with her interrogation, placing a hand in front of Alexandria to keep her from moving too close to Josephine. She seemed weary and her voice slurred and dragged. "That isn't secret information. If you want to be recognized by the council of heroes, we need more information, like your name."

"I've never heard of this council."

"It's new." Brites shrugged. Alexandria thought she seemed

incredibly disinterested, tucked in her small, shadowy corner of the room. "We established it after the Amazon-Hunter war. As the hero of Athena, you'll be granted a seat at the council– *if* Athena relents in her ambitions to take over Olympia, that is. Until then, unfortunately, you're considered treasonous to Olympia and therefore can't be given a seat."

"I'm *saving* Olympia."

"That's what everyone who's ever been a traitor to Olympia has said," Wen-Tang snarled from a different corner of the room where she flipped her knife. "I'm sure Athena has told you the story of Atar? He was the greatest traitor to Olympia that anyone has ever known, and he swore it was for the good of the heroes that he killed all the gods. I was there when it happened. And then Keilee swore she was trying to keep the Amazons and the Hunters safe during the Amazon-Hunter war, but she killed Sophia, Artemis' Hunter."

There was a brief pause. Brites made a small gesture with her hand and muttered something under her breath that Alexandria couldn't make out. The pained expression on her face was clear, however: it was still not safe to mention Sophia in front of her. *Now's really not the time,* Alexandria thought. *We can't get anything done.*

Athena's Warrior picked up on the change in the mood of the room as well. Her eyes narrowed at Brites and then flashed towards Wen-Tang. Alexandria saw the calculations running through her mind. They were evident in the clear grey eyes.

"You're simply too stupid to see it," the Warrior said. "Olympia is in chaos and constantly at war with itself. Were Athena to come to power, she would stop such madness. There would be peace in Olympia that would last as long as the gods and nevermore would we have to worry about defending our borders or diplomacy between peoples. And! We would regain our preeminence among the mortals. Once again, we'd be worshipped and adored– we would have the run of the land, as much food and drink as we wanted. The old rest stops would be brought back to life and would bustle with adventurers trekking the world, gaining knowledge and experience. Entire cities would be at our command. The gods would matter once more, and we would supervise temples erected in their names. Does that not sound exciting? Does that not sound wonderful?"

It was a compelling argument, perhaps, were it made to a different audience. But the Warrior had not realized who she was speaking to, or at the very least, she had miscalculated the issue. Alexandria was the hero of Ares. She would never give up war entirely, nor wish to live in a land entirely peaceful. Her existence was brought to fruition when she stood on the front lines; Alexandria knew that the moment she stood in front of an army ready to defend Olympia, she would feel complete.

And the other heroes were forged warriors, battered by years of skirmishes and battles. Even Triniya and Jasmin, the gentlest of the ones in the room, had struggled in the Hunter-Amazon war, though not as much as the others. No, an appeal to the prospects of peace would not satisfy them.

"Maybe that would've worked with other mortals," she said, a sharp edge to her voice. "But all of us bear the sword just as easily as we bear crowns. Are the Warriors of Athena so loath to pick up their own weapons? Then we could just meet them on the battlefield; we will have an easy time defeating them."

"How dare you!" the Warrior scowled at her. "We would beat you on any battlefield in the world!"

"That is the Queen of the Amazons you are speaking to," Wen-Tang interrupted, scowling furiously. "Do not be so hasty to make such wild claims. Even at the height of her strength, Athena never succeeded in defeating the Amazons in pitched combat. I doubt that has changed."

"Let's try and stay on topic," Jasmin interjected, rubbing her forehead. "We don't have time to argue about who would win a fight or not. What's your name?" she asked again.

The Warrior glared at them and blurted, "Josephine," and then she pressed her lips in a thin line as if she hadn't meant to reveal that information at all.

"Thank you," Jasmin replied. "Here's the deal, Josephine. We're not going to let you go back to Athena, that would be stupid. It would put us at risk. We also, however, don't have time to be dragging a prisoner around the world as we try and chase down Athena again. Nor do we have a prison we can throw you in for the time being as we decide what to do with you."

"As you can see, we're in a bit of a bind." Triniya nodded. She leaned back into her chair, which seemed to swallow her with its size.

"Yes," Jasmin continued. "There's no easy solution, but I've thought of two options and I'm going to let you pick one, Josephine." Alexandria frowned; they had not discussed any of this but none of the heroes argued with Jasmin. They needed to show some kind of united front. Wen-Tang fingered her knife slowly and caught Jasmin's eye, but the oracle simply frowned and shook her head.

"Killing you isn't one of the options, either. We have some responsibility to the other heroes, Wen-Tang. So, Josephine, here's my offer: you can help us, and we'll protect you in front of the gods, or we can bring you back to Olympia and prosecute you."

Alexandria's frown deepened. That seemed like a waste of Josephine's potential usefulness. She would be an asset as they wandered around Warrior strongholds and tried to locate information. With a little force, Josephine might even be compelled to release secrets or identify fake documents.

She started ever so slightly. She wanted to use *force* on Josephine, force her to do what Alexandria wished for her. A darkness seemed to hang over her every thought. *I'm angry. And I don't know why.*

Josephine eyed the heroes as she considered. Alexandria focused her gaze on the prisoner, pushing away the thoughts in her mind. This was no time for such ideas; there was work to be done and a country to preserve.

"I'll come with you," Josephine finally decided.

She probably thinks it's a better shot at escaping, Alexandria thought. *At least she won't be locked up. Maybe we can get something out of her.*

"Then swear you will not betray us," Wen-Tang said before Jasmin had a chance to utter another word. She took a step forward. "An oath. I won't travel with her if she doesn't," she turned to Jasmin and Triniya. "I refuse to put myself at risk for no reason."

"Wen-Tang is right," Jasmin agreed. "Swear an oath, Josephine, and we'll bring you with us. Who knows? Maybe we can convince you to dissuade Athena from her plan."

Josephine snorted, staring Jasmin down. Alexandria watched the tense competition, eyes flitting between the two girls.

"I swear as the hero of Athena and her Warrior that I will not betray you while I am with you or while this conflict continues," Josephine finally said, slowly enunciating her words. "Does that oath satisfy you?"

The girls look between each other and exchanged shrugs or nods. "For now," Wen-Tang agreed. "It's getting late. We should turn in for the night. We have to get an early start tomorrow if we're heading all the way to Egypt."

Egypt? Alexandria's head swiveled towards Wen-Tang. *Why would we be heading to Egypt?*

Brites leaned forward and said to Alexandria. "Remember what the ghost from the Underworld said? Something is happening in the library of Alexandria. That's the best lead we've got at the moment, so we're heading there tomorrow morning. Athena might be hiding something in the ruins of it since no one would think to look there."

"Then, to bed we go," Jasmin said. "I could frankly do with some sleep. I feel exhausted after all of those ghosts."

"I hear ya." Triniya clapped a hand on Jasmin's shoulder. "Underworld journeys really suck the life out of ya, don't they?"

"Ha ha," Wen-Tang muttered, standing up and moving towards the door. "Goodnight."

Her disappearance to one of the bedrooms was the signal for everyone to disperse for the night. Only Josephine was left in that bedroom, and Brites locked the door behind her. Even after an oath, they would take only the necessary liberties.

INTERLUDE
THE ROOFS OF KAVALA

Day 5

The soft wind chilled Alexandria's cheeks. She twisted her hands on the ornate metal railings of the hotel roof and stared out at the few lights of the city. It was so late that even the Greek parties had dispersed by this time and the restaurant lights fizzled out one by one, plunging the city into an ever-deeper darkness. Her mind whirled with everything that had transpired over the past day and she found sleep impossible. There was the Underworld and Hades and her supposed betrayal of the other heroes. There was Athena attempting to kill her and failing, presumably because of her connection with Ares.

She replayed the scene in her head over and over. She picked up the edges of her red chlamys and ran her fingers over the fabric. It was supple and soft, the way it had always been. It did not seem like it would be able to repel a sword. But in the moment, Alexandria swore it had hardened to something akin to armour. Like it had been spurred to action by the strike.

It's not impossible. The sword of Penthesilea flashed in her mind. Olympia was full of weird and wonderful– and very dangerous– artifacts of magic, imbued with the power of the gods. That her chlamys had been altered by Ares was not unlikely.

"What are you thinking about?" Wen-Tang stepped next to her and leaned her hands against the railings, looking down at the street and the trickling of the last few drunks home. "Couldn't sleep?"

Alexandria shook her head tersely. "No. You?"

"Not at all," Wen-Tang sighed. Whatever anger she'd held against Alexandria seemed dissipated, gone. Like it had just been a blip in their friendship. "I'm too nervous about bringing Josephine along to rest comfortably. She was far too eager to make that oath; she has some loophole concerning it that I'm not aware of. I know it. Those Warriors are sly tricksters. Heroes take on the attributes of their gods– you'll see. You haven't noticed the changes yet, but I see more of Ares in you every day. You're more reckless... idiotic. Don't try and argue with me. I know you are; you're impulsive with every decision you make. You've stepped into your own as the Queen of the Amazons, sure, but you've also truly become the hero of Ares. I've noticed it in myself too, since becoming the princess of Atlantis. I feel angrier, like there's power in my body that needs to be released but can't be. I don't know what to do about it..."

"Why would you have to do anything about it?" Alexandria asked, furrowing her brow. "If it's inevitable, why wouldn't you just embrace it?"

Wen-Tang shook her head. Her knuckles turned white as she grasped the iron harder. "I'm telling you this in confidence, okay? I need to tell someone, or it's going to drive me crazy." A strange laugh came out of her. "You can't tell anyone what I just said, not even the other heroes. I can't say for sure if it's true or not, I have no real proof beyond what I've read, but I've had suspicions for a long time. I don't want them to think I'm unfit to finish this mission."

"Why would you tell me?" Alexandria raised an eyebrow, staring at the other girl. A moment of intense silence elapsed between the two of them as they measured themselves against each other.

"I was angry with you," Wen-Tang said finally. "I still want you to explain what contact you've had with Athena– don't think I'll forget about that– but you are also my friend, Alexandria. I owe you my life and I will recognize the bond that creates between us."

Alexandria was surprised by what Wen-Tang said. She hadn't thought the pirate would forgive her any time soon, no matter what happened on the beach between them and Ares. "Thank you. So your secret..."

"Yes," Wen-Tang turned around and leaned her lower back against the railing, her head tilted to look at Alexandria who slowly pulled her gaze away from the deadening town in front of her. "I know Triniya explained to you how the gods forge history. That's where my suspicions begin. Officially, there are no records kept of how things were before the gods intervened–"

"Triniya mentioned that–"

"Don't interrupt, please. The longer this takes to tell you, the more danger I'm putting the both of us in."

Alexandria was about to retort but the slightly scared look in Wen-Tang's eyes gave her pause. She never imagined the pirate as scared of anything; rather, Wen-Tang seemed to charge recklessly into all sorts of danger without a moment's hesitation. It was something she'd always admired about the pirate. She nodded her head.

"Thank you. As I was saying, officially, there are no records. The mortals certainly couldn't keep any, and the only gods who would have been interested– Athena and Apollo– were expressly forbidden from writing any of it down. Hell, they were often in charge of cleaning up mortal records and erasing history. As far as I can tell, they never bothered to disobey that order... but I was roaming the libraries in Atlantis and I found this tucked-away chest in a corner that looked like it had been untouched and unopened for millennia. Naturally, I was curious, and since no one was going to stop the Princess of Atlantis from doing whatever she pleased, I took the chest back with me to my room and opened it.

"I'm sure you can guess what I found. Dozens and dozens of records of different events that happened in the mortal world and were overturned or changed by the gods. But not just in the mortal world," Wen-Tang's voice lowered, and her eyes darted back and forth warily. "The gods have been interfering with the history of Olympia before the destruction. Your predecessor, Penthesilea, was not the last Queen of the Amazons. There was a girl named Alcippe who was crowned right before the destruction– and then during the final battles, she was shepherded away to the mortal realm again and Penthesilea was brought back to improve morale. I don't know what became of Alcippe, but that's beside the point. What's more interesting, at least in my opinion, is why Penthesilea was deposed by Ares at all.

"The writing was slightly convoluted but the gist of it was that she had grown too unstable. She was channeling too much of Ares' personality and characteristics– essentially, she was becoming a little too godlike for a mortal body to handle– and it became dangerous for Olympia. She couldn't be given power because the risk that she would incite a war or attack a mortal country was too high. She must have been barely functioning during the final battle... and I don't know if you've heard the story of Atar."

Alexandria shook her head wordlessly, mind reeling from everything that Wen-Tang had just told her.

"That's a story for another time. Suffice it to say that during the final battle, he turned on all the gods and killed them. The papers I found say it's because he had become too much like Zeus. His mind wasn't able to accommodate it, and it drove him mad. He's still alive, you know, he fled to the North, past your fortress and the mountain range. Like Penthesilea did, he must have recovered once he stopped being Zeus' hero. Anyway," Wen-Tang took a breath and grabbed Alexandria's hand. "My point is: the power of the gods drives us heroes mad, apparently."

Alexandria's breath hitched in her throat. "What do you mean, exactly?"

"What I said." Wen-Tang shrugged. "We're all doomed. Have been since we took on the mantles of heroes. It's just a matter of time before their power overwhelms us. The more powerful the god, the faster it happens. My time is coming." She turned and looked out at the city again, refusing to meet Alexandria's eyes. "I can feel it– I know it's not paranoia. Taking the crown of Atlantis heightened it. Everything seems too much now. I want to fight everyone around me; to implode."

"How do you know those records are true?" Alexandria whispered. "You don't know who wrote them."

"No, I don't. I doubt it was Poseidon. I think it was another hero, someone close to the gods who was observing what happened. Why and how the documents made their way to Atlantis, I have no idea. I don't know if Poseidon is aware of their existence."

Silence fell between them as if Wen-Tang was struggling to continue speaking. Alexandria brushed her hair out of her face and waited patiently. Her mind reeled with everything Wen-

Tang was saying and she couldn't parse her fear from logic. This was a wild claim. The gods had no reason to destroy their own heroes, especially not after working so hard to train them. It would be in their best interest to have heroes that lasted for centuries.

If it was true that the power of the gods corrupted the minds of the heroes, then why had people like Sophia and Jasmin lasted as long as they had? Eyeing Wen-Tang, Alexandria pursed her lips. How had Wen-Tang survived this long? She had no idea how many years ago Poseidon had chosen her, but Wen-Tang knew stories from before the destruction. *At the very least, it's been a long time.*

"I can feel it," Wen-Tang whispered. "I know it's true because everything described in those scrolls is something I feel or... I just know it."

"I don't know." Alexandria pushed away the surging reminders of the darkness that seemed to envelop her limbs now. Wen-Tang was making her paranoid. There was no reason to believe that the heavy feeling in her heart related to this: it was probably just homesickness or adjustment or the effects of her position as a hero. *Nothing else.*

"I've escaped it this long because for half of the time I've been Poseidon's hero, he hasn't been around feeding me his power. There was a pause after the destruction where the heroes weren't under any influence... it extended our lives, I think." Wen-Tang inhaled sharply, her face turning white with fear. Alexandria grabbed her shoulder.

Wen-Tang suddenly seemed to realize that Alexandria was still there. She composed her face and forced a smile. "It's too much to explain. It doesn't concern you, anyhow. It won't happen to you for a long time."

"You've told me all of this, but now you won't talk to me about it?"

"Not tonight." Wen-Tang looked up at the sky and the

moon. "The morning draws near and it's always best not to speak of the darker things during the rising sun. Besides, you should try and get some sleep. It would do you good. We have a busy day tomorrow. And you won't want to miss the sights of Egypt."

Alexandria frowned, but before she had the chance to argue, Wen-Tang slipped back inside, leaving her alone on the roof. With a heavy step, Alexandria also returned to her room, ruminating over everything she had learned. However much Wen-Tang had entrusted to her, there was more being kept from her. She had no idea if any of it was true, or what to make of it. She kicked off her boots and lay down on the bed.

Closing her eyes, she was inundated with images of Wen-Tang going mad. The faces shifted through all of the people she'd met in Olympia until she saw her own face, insane with rage and hatred, cutting down people– and even gods– left and right. Her sword seemed to flash red, and her eyes were brighter than even Ares'. The other heroes screamed at her to stop, to not fall to the darkness, but Alexandria ignored them all. The only emotion she felt was insatiable anger: it was as if the darkness in her heart had taken over her faculties.

Alexandria woke up trying not to scream.

The sun streamed through the window in her room, and Alexandria rested her head back on the pillow, wondering how long she'd managed to sleep. If she listened carefully and held her breath, she could hear the pattering of Jasmin and Triniya downstairs as they made their cups of coffee. Their voices floated up the staircase, but too indistinctly for her to parse what they were saying. Then, she heard Wen-Tang's voice interrupting sharply and silence fell upon the house. With that, Alexandria stood up.

She pulled her boots back onto her feet and padded down the stairs without trying to be quiet. She didn't care. It wasn't true, it couldn't be. She was not in danger of becoming prey to madness. Wen-Tang was mistaken; she was just stressed and worried about her new role as the Princess of Atlantis. There were more important things to worry about today, like going to Egypt. Yes, that's what she needed to focus on.

"Good morning," she said, entering the kitchen.

CHAPTER 8
ALEXANDRIA, EGYPT

Day 7

It was not at all how Josephine had remembered it from the last time. There were no sand dunes picturesquely dotting the horizon, nor any massive temples and monuments for her to peer at and appreciate. It was dirty and busy and crowded, and the heroes were in a rush to reach the hidden entrance to the library. The entire city rested on the coastline, against the sparkling blue waters. All the buildings seemed whitewashed and icy, warmed only by the beating glares of the sun and the scent of human sweat and breath crowding around her. Just a year ago, Josephine would never have imagined being in Egypt again, after her last time in the Library.

Brites stuck close to her side. Josephine found her less intolerable than the others. She was quiet and controlled and didn't chatter away like Triniya, whom she despised, or even Jasmin, who for all her knowledge and wisdom, grated on Josephine's nerves. Wen-Tang and Alexandria walked ahead of everyone else, lost in a heated conversation. Those two she liked the least. They were haughty and prideful and looked down upon Athena's Warriors.

She only caught snippets of their discussion, but it was clear that Alexandria was pressing for information that Wen-Tang did not wish to reveal. A small smile crept onto her face. Athena had been correct; there was dissension among the heroes. They could not put aside the petty grudges that had developed between their gods. It trickled down into their followers. The Warriors couldn't possibly lose to such scattered loyalties when their own were iron-clad.

"What are you thinking?" Brites asked, looking ahead at Wen-Tang and Alexandria. "Don't mind them. They're discussing some book that Wen-Tang found or something."

Josephine turned her head to look at the girl. Her explanation was too hasty and too simple to be true. She knew that Josephine was observing something she shouldn't be, and Brites was trying to mitigate its consequences. Alexandria and Wen-Tang weren't bookworms, that was clear. They'd never argue over a book.

"I'm sure," Josephine answered in a measured tone. "I am a hero, too, you know. I have also been privy to the histories of the gods. I can tell that whatever their issue is lies with the gods, and not with some novel."

"Why did you take that oath?" Brites changed the subject. Josephine's eyes narrowed. *So it does have to do with the gods. And Brites doesn't wish me to hear it. That's not much information, unfortunately.*

"What do you mean?"

"You swore an oath not to betray us without hesitation," Brites elaborated. "That was either a very calculated decision and you know a way out of the oath that I can't see, or your allegiance to Athena has been fake this entire time. I don't think you're pretending to be Athena's hero, so I believe you've found a loophole in the oath, and I want to know what it is."

"If I did, why would I tell you?"

"I don't know. Because your oath might require you to tell me if you are planning anything that might put us in danger? I could hold you to it, Josephine."

Josephine closed her eyes and then opened them again, looking straight ahead. "If I am taken by force by the Warriors, then I can be compelled by them to work for Athena again. My oath will not hold if it is technically forced betrayal; and once you are defeated, I will be freed of its bounds. We are heading straight into a large Warriors complex. That they will let me leave with you seems unlikely, Brites, don't you think?"

Brites stopped, spun, and grabbed her arm. "If you think I will let you put our mission in danger, you are mistaken, Josephine. Jasmin doesn't want us to kill you but if it is between you and us, I will not hesitate. I have lost too many friends over the years to take a risk with you."

Josephine pulled her arm away. "You cannot stand against the Warriors of Athena. You're simply kidding yourselves if you think you have a chance."

Brites scoffed.

"Are you two okay back there?" Jasmin asked. Everyone huddled around in the middle of the street, forcing other passerby to cut around them. Josephine and Brites glared at each other and then looked at Jasmin.

"We're fine," Josephine said.

"No, we're not," Brites snapped. "She intends to betray us as soon as we get to the library."

A clamour of voices broke out and everyone crowded around Josephine, shouting both at her and at everyone else present. All except for Wen-Tang, who stood at the edge of the gathering, watching, calculating, a menacing glare in her eyes. Josephine caught it and shuddered. There was something evil and dangerous in the Pirate's stance, and it did not solely pertain to Athena or the Warriors. Something much darker seemed afoot.

Before she could contemplate any longer, Alexandria grabbed Josephine's shoulder. She didn't speak, but held Josephine tightly, watching the others calm down and silence settle.

"We can't deal with this here," Alexandria decided. "People are staring."

"We can't wait until after we enter the library," Brites shot back, her eyes narrowing at Wen-Tang. "We can't bring Josephine anywhere near the other Warriors."

Wen-Tang finally spoke up, her fists clenched at her side. She seemed to be fighting to control herself. Josephine cocked her head and observed carefully as the Pirate slowly loosened her fists and her posture relaxed. "I say we leave her and Jasmin in a hotel room and the rest of us deal with the library. Jasmin's the most adept with oaths and might be able to remedy Josephine's slip."

"I don't see any issue with that," Jasmin said. "I can hammer something out, I'm sure. Even though I really did want to see the library, destroyed or not," she added under her breath.

Josephine smiled. It wouldn't be difficult at all to convince Jasmin to leave the hotel room. There were far too many interesting artifacts and old scrolls for an Oracle of Apollo to resist.

"Then we'll split here," Wen-Tang continued. "And find you after we get what we want."

"Stay in touch." Jasmin nodded, grabbing Josephine's hand.

Alexandria slowly relinquished her grasp and stepped to the side, allowing the two of them to pass through and cross the street, heading for the nearest hotel. Everyone else fell back into formation and let Wen-Tang lead the way to the old entrance to the library.

"That wasn't a smart idea," Triniya informed Wen-Tang once they had begun walking again. "Jasmin's now alone with Josephine, who won't have any qualms about trying to escape."

"Jasmin can hold her own," Wen-Tang scowled. "And if anyone has a chance to convince Josephine to forego her madness, it's the other bookworm of the group."

Alexandria trailed behind them, listening intently. She didn't agree with the split either, but like Wen-Tang, she saw its benefit. It was one less wild card to deal with. *Besides*, Alexandria thought as she watched Wen-Tang's straight black hair swish from side to side, *no one else offered to take charge of the situation.*

Well, I would have. The dark and heavy sensation rose in her chest again and Alexandria forced herself not to clutch at her skin. It was not the skin or the bones, but something much, much deeper. She briefly wondered if it was her body beginning to decay from godly forces, if she was going mad the way Wen-Tang believed all of them inevitably would.

It's far too soon, she reminded herself. *Wen-Tang has been serving Poseidon for decades and only now believes the effects are beginning to show. I have only just begun. I've got many, many years ahead of me before I have to worry about insanity.*

Still, the weight in her chest did not dissipate. It tightened its hold on her lungs and heart, and her throat began to malfunction, like she couldn't swallow anymore. For a second, she stopped walking, trying to regain control of her limbs and body. And as soon as it came, it passed, and the world was bright and noisy again. The other heroes had not noticed her pause and she jogged to catch up with them, falling in beside Brites once more.

"This whole expedition is turning into a mess," Brites muttered to her after they had walked on in silence for a time.

"We've jumped around the Mediterranean to no avail, and we don't really seem to have a goal in mind. We can't attack Athena on the scant evidence we have, but we won't force Josephine to give us anything better. We're just chasing phantoms. As long as they know we're coming, they'll keep destroying their plans, changing them, or giving us fake ones to throw us off. We ought to just fight Athena head-on. Or bring Josephine back to Olympia for questioning."

Alexandria hummed, pursing her lips, turning left with the rest of the girls, and almost running straight into a group of chatty young women. She sidestepped to avoid them, slipping by with a forced smile. "I see what you mean. But I don't think we have much of a choice. We're not going to beat Athena in hand-to-hand combat, especially not if there's a backup of Warriors with her. The council of gods won't act unless we give them proof of Athena's plans... I don't think there's a better way than what we've come up with."

"If we forced Josephine..."

"She has the same status as us," Alexandria interrupted. She was beginning to lose track of where they were. The route that Brites and Wen-Tang led them on meandered through shortcuts and alleyways, cutting right and left and doubling back on itself. It was impossible to tell where in the city they were, how far they'd walked, or any such thing. All of the buildings had the same washed sand colour to them, or else they were white with faded blue roofs that must have been brilliant cobalt once. "We can't torture information out of her; that's insane. She's not our enemy, Athena is. The same way I wasn't your enemy during the Hunter-Amazon war."

She was trying to convince herself, as well. The urge tugged at her. *We could solve everything, so easily. This whole fiasco would be over and we could return to Olympia in triumph. No one has to die. Josephine isn't even really one of us–* but Alexandria forced herself to resist the temptation. She thought back to Ares and the sword of Penthesilea. How outraged the gods had been about the mind-control. *I can't. I won't sully my time as a hero by that. I'm not like the gods. I care about the other heroes–*

"You were my enemy," Brites stated, matter-of-factly.

"Not enough for someone to assassinate me or anything like that. We have to have honour, or we're no better than Keilee and her like. We shouldn't put all the blame on her; Josephine's been tricked by Athena, I'm sure of it. I mean, I certainly didn't know about the sword of Penthesilea until it was too late."

"It's different." Brites shook her head.

"How?" Alexandria tried not to smile as she looked away from Brites' face to recompose herself. A sunburn had already begun to form on Brites' nose, turning it pink. *It's not even that sunny out.* It wasn't, really– there were clouds dotting the sky and the sea breeze made it feel much cooler than it was. But Alexandria was used to hotter climates. Olympia, for all its warmth, was a cloudy land, and Brites had not left it in a long time. *Funny that a half-nymph is affected by the sun.*

"I don't know," Brites replied. "It just is. I can feel the malevolence in her. You didn't know anything about Olympia or the gods when you came, but Athena definitely didn't keep her hero in the dark like that. Josephine knows things. She knows about the destruction and the people who were involved. I can tell because of the way she looks at Wen-Tang and me. You were so ignorant, you couldn't be held culpable for all that you did. I don't think Josephine has the same excuse."

"We'll have to finish this conversation later," Alexandria said as she glanced at their other companions ahead of them. "It looks like we're here."

The place seemed dejected, a forgotten corner of a forgotten city, unkempt and wild from years of weeds growing through cobblestone. Unlike the rest of the city, which buzzed with life and vitality, it was cold and deserted. No sunlight trickled into the deep refuges of the place.

The other two girls had paused in front of this unassuming side street that dead-ended. Brites and Alexandria joined them, and Wen-Tang nodded towards a darker-coloured stone in the masonry.

"It's just through here. Before we go in, we should have a plan for what we're going to do."

"Not get distracted," Alexandria suggested.

"Very funny," Wen-Tang snorted. "We'll split up into two groups? Cover as much distance as possible and look for any plans that might be related to Olympia. If things go south–"

"They will," Brites muttered. "They always do."

"Then we'll meet at the hotel where Jasmin and Josephine are. This place is so large I doubt we'll run into that many Warriors, unless it's crawling with them. Brites, you're with Alexandria since she doesn't know the area and you've been here the most. Triniya and I will stay together."

Everyone assented in various forms and Wen-Tang stepped forward to open the door to the Library of Alexandria. The stones shuddered as they shifted and opened up only just wide enough for one person to squeeze in at a time. One by one, the heroes passed through, and just as Alexandria stepped forward, the stones shuddered again and closed behind them, sealing them into the living tomb of the Library of Alexandria, once the pride of the ancient world.

CHAPTER 9
THE LIBRARY OF ALEXANDRIA

Day 7

It had retained much of its former glory. Or at least, Alexandria assumed it had once looked very similar to this, when it was above ground and a thriving hub of learning and discovery. Massive marble columns held up hundreds of shelves laden with yellowing scrolls piled haphazardly into their containers. The whole place hummed with life. A faint glow appeared to emanate from the various bookshelves, like hints of sunlight peering through scrolls. A shimmer floated in the air, rendering the whole thing into a dreamscape, giving it an ethereal quality that Alexandria could not describe.

"I thought the Library of Alexandria had been destroyed," Alexandria whispered.

Brites hummed. "It was. I watched it be destroyed. This is the rebuilt version. It used to be nicer, trust me."

Alexandria frowned. "These manuscripts look like the originals. I wonder how much work it took to dig them all out of the ashes."

"It's *beautiful*," Triniya said, her jaw agape. "I don't see how it ever could have been nicer."

Alexandria's breath hitched as she looked down at the floors. They were not the white, creamy marble color that the rest of the building was. The entire floor, as far as she could see, was covered in delicate mosaics of blue and green and gold. She crouched down and ran her hand over the bumpy edges of the glass shards. Some of the stories she was able to pick out: there was Athena and Arachne, who'd had the hubris to assume she was better than the goddess. There were mosaics of big temples and large festivals, just as Alexandria had pictured they might be in Ancient Greece.

And there were other stories painted into the tile that Alexandria didn't know, though she could guess at some of them. There was the destruction, she was sure, underneath a newer bookshelf. A council of either heroes or younger-looking gods– she could not tell which– was depicted next to it. Hundreds of other depictions drew her attention here and there, but Brites grabbed her arm and pulled her back up.

"There are far nicer ones on Olympus," she said. "And we have a task. You cannot be distracted."

"I'm not," Alexandria replied, wondering when she'd get the chance to see the ones on Olympus. "Where do we start?"

"Follow me. Athena won't be foolish enough to store her plans, or her people, in the accessible part of the library. It's still in use and there'll be people in and out of it too frequently."

"Who uses it?" Alexandria asked as they began walking on the left-hand side, breaking away from Wen-Tang and Triniya. "I thought after the destruction, no one left Olympia."

"You don't think we're the only ones with gods, do you?" Brites laughed. She pointed to a young woman dressed in a white tunic, her dark hair pulled back by a golden circlet. She was rummaging through a pile of scrolls. The clasps on her dress were in the shape of scarabs and Alexandria briefly recalled learning about the Egyptians and their obsession with beetles.

"Egyptian?"

"The Egyptian gods are very real and a constant pain to deal with. They hate the Greek gods who took over their worshippers– because while we have Olympia, they don't have a country of their own. They never had enough power to create one, so they've remained bound to the mortal world. Mostly to the pyramids. We rarely interact with them – it usually ends in bloodshed. Their followers are nice enough, though. They might have been the ones to resuscitate the Library... it was probably one of their archives from the Pyramids that they just moved back here after the burning."

The young Egyptian caught their eyes. Her eyebrows raised as she looked them up and down and noticed the Greek symbols on their chlamyses.

"Anx weda seneb," Brites bowed low. "We mean no harm. We are here on official Olympia business, but we promise not to disturb your research."

"Anx weda seneb. Well-met, Brites, child of Artemis. Your kindness in the past has not been forgotten and your presence is welcome in the Library." The other girl bowed as well. "Who is your companion?"

"This is Alexandria, the new hero of Ares." Brites waved Alexandria over. She bowed. "I vouch for her conduct."

"A friend of Brites is welcome here. My name is Asenath. I serve the lord Ra as a temple priestess. I trust you will find all you need in the Library, whether it be knowledge or safety."

"Nice to meet you, Asenath," Alexandria said.

Asenath hummed. "If you'll excuse me, I must return to my research. Something, or someone, has been pilfering the Library of its resources and it is causing the priestesses great distress. We are hoping one of these scrolls," she motioned to the box, "might provide us with the description of whatever ancient monster has made its way inside."

Brites hesitated, opening her mouth and then closing it again. Finally, she said, "I wish you luck, Asenath, daughter of Ra. My companion and I will be on our way. Sem em hetep."

"Sem em hetep, Brites, daughter of Artemis." Asenath turned back to her scroll without bidding farewell to Alexandria. Brites pulled her away, back into the folds of the bookshelves, and they continued walking along the perimeter, peering into doors that led into empty rooms.

"What was that about?" Alexandria asked. "Why did she call you a daughter of Artemis?"

"That's simply how they address heroes." Brites shrugged. "They don't see a distinction between a follower and a demigod."

They stopped at a dilapidated, eerie hallway. It looked like it might cave in at any moment, and a little sign at one edge of the entrance warned the priests and priestesses of its structural unsoundness. Brites narrowed her eyes at the darkness and turned back to Alexandria. "We might as well try this."

Alexandria pulled out a knife from her sheath and flipped it in her hand. "I'm ready if you are."

With a quiet chuckle, Brites pulled out a knife of her own and took the first step forward. They walked together into the darkness and the further they went, the more the darkness grew and the quieter it became, as if they were walking through a cave. At about the halfway point, a door appeared on the left-hand side. Both of them stilled. They could hear voices from behind the door, arguing about something.

"Those aren't Egyptians," Brites whispered. "They don't have the accent."

"I hear it. Warriors?"

"Probably."

Alexandria took a step closer to the door, slowly, and leaned her ear to the wood. She closed her eyes and listened for a second. The conversation seemed to sharpen and suddenly she could hear what they were saying.

"We have no choice! If they won't ally with us, we have to get rid of them!"

"We can't lay siege to the Library; that's insane. They have as much a right to it as we do!"

"If they wake their gods, they will put us all at risk. We do not have the manpower to hold them off. We would need to ally with the other gods, and there is simply no way Athena could be convinced."

Alexandria turned her head and mouthed to Brites: "Warriors." Brites' lips thinned and she looked at the door with determination. Alexandria could imagine sparks of flame in her eyes as every muscle in the Hunter's body hardened.

"Heard anything?" she mouthed back. Alexandria shook her head and turned her attention back to eavesdropping at the door.

"We cannot abandon all the work we've done here. We are still weeks, if not months, away from being prepared for a full-scale invasion. Moving all of our material and equipment to some other rest stop would put us too far behind schedule."

"What do you suggest, then?" another voice snapped back. "I bet you think you could go one-on-one with Ra or Horus, do you? Think you're of the same caliber as the heroes of old?"

"How dare you-"

"I'm not done. You've been trying to convince us to make bad decision after bad decision. You're going to get us all killed if you don't stop. You seem to think you could become another Atar and defeat the gods all on your own. Well, you can't! He was insane with power and had an army behind him– you're one of the worst fighters we have and you're certainly not Athena's hero!"

Something slammed loudly. Alexandria and Brites flinched.

"I'll have you killed for that!"

"James, take him out," another, calmer voice interrupted. Alexandria barely had time to scurry to the side of the door and hide herself in the shadows before it flew open and a young man was thrown into the hallway. He turned around but the door was shut in his face, slamming against his nose. He slid down to the bottom, clutching at the bleeding nostrils, and whimpered.

"If only you listened to me..." he breathed. "I could lead us to the most glorious of victories..."

Alexandria blinked and suddenly, the boy was gasping and shaking as Brites' knife pressed against his throat, daring him to move or speak. For all of the anger that Alexandria could read in Brites' stance and her muscles, her face was serenely calm, and she observed her victim with cold detachment.

"Name," she said.

The young man simply whimpered again and shook his head slightly. Brites pressed closer with the tip of the blade, drawing a drop of blood. He stilled.

"Name. I'm not in a mood to play games."

"Frederick," he replied after a brief pause. "I'm nothing special, please- I'll tell you everything I know if you promise to let me go- the people you want are the ones inside! I can get you back in! I'll tell you who you need to capture! I'll do anything! Please don't kill me!"

"Whether or not you live is entirely up to how you conduct yourself," Brites replied coldly. "I have enough blood on my hands. What's one more? And you hardly seem that difficult, you sniveling coward. You're certainly not worthy to be called a Warrior of Athena."

"I-"

"I despise traitors." Brites crouched down so that their eyes were at the same level. Alexandria watched with bated breath as the exchange continued, as Brites seemed to toy with Frederick's mind and life. She had never seen the Hunter act this way; since she had arrived in Olympia, Brites had almost seemed out of place next to Sophia, Artemis' old hero. She was warm and kind and though she was fierce, she was never terrifying the way Priya and Keilee were. There was a softness in her gaze and demeanour that belied the apparent danger underneath. Alexandria wondered if Sophia's death had anything to do with it or if Brites had always been this cold, and she'd simply never seen it.

"What would your fellow Warriors think about the fact that you were so willing to sell them out? Without a second thought, you were prepared to give me names and to point out your leaders in order to spare your own skin. Honestly, I'd be doing Athena a favour if I killed you for her. One less weakling that would buckle at the mere thought of dying."

"I didn't– I'm one of her most useful cartographers!"

"Cartographer," Brites scoffed. "Because map-makers win wars, yes, I forgot."

"Why-" Frederick suddenly seemed to gain some strength and indignation from Brites' mockery. Without regard for the knife pressing threateningly into his skin, he shouted, "Invaders outside!"

"Shut up, Frederick!" came a voice from within.

"Heroes from Olympia!" He tried once more before Brites clamped her hand over his mouth.

The same voice from behind the door answered, "We're not letting you back in; it's not worth trying to trick us into opening the door!"

"Mm," Brites whispered in his ear. "You seem indispensable to them, don't you? Tell me, what is Athena planning to do in Olympia? When? You've clearly been present at meetings. You must have a sense of your goddess's plans. I want them. Now."

Another trickle of blood from his neck. Humiliated, tears

ran down Frederick's face as he divulged every secret and every plan he was privy to. Alexandria listened with fascination as Brites wrung all she could from him, forcing him to clarify every point and double-checking his story occasionally. She seemed to be well-practiced in the arts of acquiring information. Alexandria wondered how common that had been in the centuries before the destruction.

"Well," Brites finally stood up and said, "I think you've given us all that you can. But now remains the question: what should we do with you? You're a liability, Frederick. We wouldn't want you telling the other Warriors that you've given away confidential information. Then they might change their plans. But I'd rather not leave a body lying around. That would be rude to the priestesses who maintain the temples. They like me so much. I'd hate to ruin my reputation."

"I won't tell anyone! Please, I'll keep it secret, they'll never know I told you anything- please don't hurt me!"

"Oh, Frederick." Brites pulled him up by the scruff of his neck. "That's just not good enough. I'm not going to kill you though, you needn't worry about that. I have a much, much better idea of what to do with you."

Alexandria followed, trying to suppress her laughter, as Brites dragged Frederick into the library and back towards Asenath, who was still rummaging through her box of scrolls.

"Anx weda seneb. I didn't mean to interrupt your work again, Asenath," Brites greeted her once more, shoving Fredrick to his knees on the floor. "But I have someone you and your priestesses might wish to deal with. I would bring him back to Olympia for prosecution, but my paths do not tend in that direction for some time, and he has sinned as grievously against you as against I."

A spark lit in Asenath's eyes as she put down her scrolls and looked down at Frederick. "What crimes has he committed?"

Alexandria could feel the Egyptian's excitement as Brites

told her about Frederick's plan to attack and steal the library on behalf of Athena. *She must not get that many chances to condemn Greek heroes.*

"Those indeed are all crimes worthy of a council against him." Asenath bowed her head, trying to hide the gleeful smile on her face. Alexandria smirked and then turned to the side, trying to mask her own expression. *Poor Frederick indeed. Not even his own people wanted him and now his capturers are laughing about putting him on the trial.* "Leave him with me. I will ensure that the other priestesses and priests are informed and that a council is immediately summoned to handle his fate. Thank you, again, for your service to us, Brites. You are a true friend of our people. In times of need, you may always seek our aid, and we will be happy to assist you."

"Thank you," Brites said. "I do not mean to leave your company so hastily, but I must return to my own. Frederick has provided me with much information that is crucial to the safety of Olympia, and it is best if the other heroes are informed soon."

"I understand," Asenath agreed. She took Frederick by the shoulder and turned her gaze back to Brites. "I hope our paths will cross again soon."

"As do I," Brites said. "Sem em hetep."

"Sem em hetep."

And the two groups split; Asenath and Frederick heading up a staircase deeper into the library and Brites and Alexandria making their way to the exit. Alexandria craned her neck, searching for any signs of Wen-Tang and Triniya amidst the shelves. But she couldn't find them. Either they were too deep into the Library, or they had already made their way back to the hotel. Alexandria shrugged and fell into conversation with Brites over Frederick's revelations. There would be time enough to worry about Wen-Tang and Triniya. The heroes had not planned to wait for each other in the Library after all.

INTERLUDE
THE EGYPTIAN TUNNELS

Day 7

"Well," Triniya said. "This is a crappy situation."

Wen-Tang kicked at the rusted bottom of the iron bars separating them from the stairs, and thus, freedom. "You're telling me."

"I didn't see that coming."

"Oh, really? No? How on earth didn't you predict that we'd get caught and jailed by Egyptian priests?"

"I don't appreciate that tone," Triniya grumbled. "It's not my fault that they thought we were hostile. You had your sword out and it's been years since we've interacted with them. They probably thought we were Athena's Warriors– I bet they suspect them of having a lair here."

"We don't have time for this." Wen-Tang kicked the bars again. "Hello? Is anyone out there?" she shouted.

Triniya leaned back against the sandy walls. "Not much we

can do about it, unfortunately. I could turn into a sparrow and fly out, but you'd still be stuck here so that's pointless because I see no set of keys lying about."

"He took them with him," Wen-Tang said. "Where did he say he was going, again?"

"To find his superior, or something," Triniya answered. "I was too busy listening to you argue with him to catch much. I don't think they'll be that long, though, and then we can explain the misunderstanding and be on our way. We should probably just leave when we do. I don't want to risk getting caught again– and getting killed on sight."

"You're right. It was clearly a stupid idea to split up. We have no idea if Brites and Alexandria are in another cell somewhere or whether they've managed to evade notice. What if we get back to the hotel and they're not there? Then we have to mount a rescue mission!"

"Wen-Tang." Triniya stood up. "You're being stupid. If they had been caught, you don't think those priests would have come back down to brag to us about having found our companions?"

"You're right." Wen-Tang slumped against the wall. "I just hate the fact that we're stuck here and can't do anything about it. If it was slightly more rotten metal, I might've been able to slice through it with my sword..."

"Nope."

"Maybe. Would have been worth a shot. But we just can't do anything until we're put before a council."

"Well, well, well, what have we caught here?" a voice said from beyond the bars.

Both Wen-Tang and Triniya peered up at the staircase and saw the ruffling of a red and white garment slowly descend. A young man appeared, wearing a long linen robe and a red linen cloak. His soft, golden eyes seemed to pierce through the shadiness of the prison tunnels. His curly dark hair was messily pulled back from his face, and around his neck, he bore a heavy golden necklace with rows of turquoise beads. A ring adorned his finger, and he carried his hand so that it was constantly visible: a scarab ring inlaid with more turquoise. His feet, peeking out from the robe, were bound by leather sandals. He looked like a young god of Olympus, who had found himself stuck in Egypt. His honey voice continued the illusion as he addressed them once more:

"What hapless circumstances have brought you to my mercy, Greeks? Once, many years ago, you would not have been brought down to these dungeons nor would I preside over a meeting to decide your fates– perhaps," he held up his hand to keep Wen-Tang from interrupting, "you think I might still honor that past with the two of you. Alas, no."

"We're not Warriors of Athena!"

"I have reason to believe you are," the young man replied. "Recently, it has come to the attention of the priests, through one of our priestesses, that there is a plot among the Warriors to take over the Library and claim it as their own, as you are surely aware, violating several millennia of agreements and treaties between our people."

"We didn't do that! We're here to stop the Warriors!"

"Be that as it may, the timing does not favour you. You were discovered minutes before we took a Warrior informant into custody from a great friend to the Egyptians, who discovered him sneaking in the hallways. We have no reason to believe that you were not an early reconnaissance force meant to discover our weaknesses and exploit them."

"Brites? Is Brites the one who gave you the informant?" Triniya said, pressing in front of Wen-Tang. "We're with her, we're part of her team."

The young man raised an eyebrow at Triniya and frowned. "Again, your statements, I cannot verify. Brites did not mention that she traveled with anyone other than the girl accompanying her. You must understand my predicament. I cannot simply let you loose when my people are in danger. For now, you will remain in the dungeons. Our council is being assembled. First, we must try the informant for his crimes, and then you will be brought before us."

He turned to leave, ignoring the two heroes as they shouted after him, trying to explain their situation. Triniya scowled and slammed her fist against the bars, but they did not yield to her strength.

The man stopped at the bottom of the stairs. His head swiveled towards them and he smiled, as if he were a cat who had finally caught his prize. Triniya watched as he looked them over, his cheeks flushed with excitement. It did not matter to him whether she and Wen-Tang were Warriors of Athena or had anything to do with them. All that mattered was that they were Greeks who had trespassed into the Library and gotten caught.

"Oh, and in case you were wondering," he said. "My name is Alex. I'm the head priest of Ra. And your lives are in my hands now."

He vanished up into the light and Triniya and Wen-Tang were once again left to their own devices. They slumped back down onto the ground. Triniya pushed a pile of sand with her foot.

"This is stupid," she grumbled. "There has to be a way to get out of this council. We can't be the first people trying to escape the Egyptians."

"We should have thought of a way to communicate with Alexandria and Brites," Wen-Tang muttered. "Maybe you should turn into a sparrow and go get the rest of the heroes."

"No," Triniya shook her head empathically. "They're waiting for an excuse to execute both of us. If I suddenly disappeared from this cell and you were left here, what do you think they'd do to you, huh?"

"We have no way of knowing they'll even come down to check."

"It's not a risk I'm willing to take," Triniya decided. "We'll have to think of some other way to get out of this mess. Gods, it would be nice if Brites would show right about now."

CHAPTER 10
A HOTEL IN ALEXANDRIA

Day 7

Jasmin sat down in front of Josephine and crossed her legs on the chair. She leaned forward slightly and stared the other girl in the face. The heavy doors of the hotel blocked all sound from coming in, muting even the flapping of the blinds in the wind. It felt like they were in an isolated world, removed from reality.

"So," Jasmin said, breaking the silence with her gentle voice. "You almost outsmarted us, Josephine. I can't say I'm surprised. Athena would never pick anyone but the brightest to be her hero. I've known a couple of them over the years, you know. The Oracles and the Warriors worked closely together before the destruction. Have you ever heard any stories about your predecessors?"

Josephine licked her lips and shook her head. Jasmin tilted her own, trying to figure out what Josephine was thinking. It was hard to read those expressionless grey eyes or the hard lines of her mouth.

"The one right before you was a boy named Thomas. His heart lay with maps and cartography, but when he needed to be, he was a skilled spear-master. Most of the time, though, it was almost impossible to drag him away from his ink-well and parchment. He created all of the topographies of Olympia that now rest in Mount Olympus' archives. He made a small one of my hometown in the mortal world for me once– I still keep it in my room."

"I'm not interested," Josephine said. "There's nothing more you could tell me about any of them that would interest me, and frankly, I'd rather you didn't try and pacify me with stories. Or try to distract me."

"I'm not–"

"You want to keep me here, in this hotel room, until your friends get back," Josephine continued as if Jasmin hadn't interrupted. "At least be honest about what you're trying to accomplish."

"Fine." Jasmin leaned back in the chair and uncrossed her legs. She surveyed Josephine with a calculating eye. "You're right. I'm keeping you here until we can decide what to do with you. What do we talk about in the meantime?"

Josephine shrugged. "Have you ever seen the Library of Alexandria?"

Jasmin nodded, her eyes glazing over as she recalled its wondrous beauty. She basked in the memories for a brief moment as they flashed before her eyes and then answered Josephine: "I have, several times, but that was long ago, before the destruction. The Oracles and the Egyptian priests were great friends at that time since we both pursued knowledge so avidly. We gifted the Library many of our scrolls and prophecies and in return, we had the run of the place whenever we wanted it..."

"It's expanded since you've last been, then," Josephine hummed. "I looked at the old schematics and the new ones. Three new wings have been added to store even more scrolls and manuscripts. And the whole tunnel system is backed up with them now. They can't build alcoves and wings fast enough at the rate work is being produced."

"Really?" Jasmin asked, peering up at Josephine with longing eyes.

"Really," Josephine said. "I could get you in to see them if you wanted. I don't know what status the Oracles hold with the Egyptians nowadays, but I do know that in the past, the Warriors of Athena had a very tenuous relation..."

"Maybe some other time," Jasmin shook her head. "I'm sure I'll get the chance to see it again someday, but duty calls and all, and I can't let you anywhere near that building. You'll turn and run the minute I do."

"I promise I won't." Josephine rolled her eyes. "I appreciate beautiful books just as much as you do, Jasmin- I would love to gaze on the library one more time before the council in Olympia sentences me back to the mortal world and erases my memories..."

Jasmin gave her a bewildered look and laughed. "Don't be silly, that's not going to happen. The council can't send a hero back to the mortal world. It would compromise the gods."

"They will force Athena to take away my title and then they will do so," Josephine replied smoothly. "I know how these things work; I have read about them in the Library."

"That's never been done–"

"You wouldn't remember, Jasmin, because they would have modified your memory too. The gods are known for doing that, aren't they? When something doesn't go their way? Once in a while, the Olympian council has one of their heroes go mad with power– mortal bodies can only handle so much godhood and it soon drives us to insanity– and they have to strip them of their title and send them back to the mortal world. I guess they live out the rest of their lives in peace with their families, none the wiser for what has occurred, though that's personal speculation."

"*You're* insane. You don't know what you're talking about. The gods could never do that; the heroes have protections in place for themselves. Besides, now we have the council of heroes and they would definitely veto any memory changing." Jasmin stood up, her face flush.

Josephine also rose and nodded towards the window. "How many times have the gods altered the history of the mortal world? A dozen? A hundred? Several thousand times? We have some of those annals kept safe in the Library, but most were never recorded or have been lost. There's no knowing if the world we live in today even remotely resembles what it should. If the gods are so willing to do that, why would they hesitate to alter their own world?"

"I don't believe it."

"Heroes are just the playthings of the gods, Jasmin. We both know that. They are trained to obey and to protect and they are given power to do so. That power slowly eats away at them until they can no longer think or act. And then, they have to be gotten rid of, in case the other heroes begin to worry or ask too many questions."

"If all of this was true," Jasmin countered, thinking of the strange shift she'd noticed in Wen-Tang's demeanor and Alexandria's tightness, "and I don't think it is, then why did you so willingly accept becoming Athena's hero?"

"I didn't know about any of this when I did," Josephine sunk back down on the chair. "Or else maybe I wouldn't have. But then again, when a god decides something, how much say do we really have? I have sworn my allegiance to Athena, and I'll serve her until the bitter end of it all, when I'm returned home with no memories, or until I die."

"That's gloomy." Jasmin's throat constricted. "I can't be sure you're telling the truth about all of this." She wrung her hands, eyeing Josephine. "It sounds outlandish and crazy, but I've watched so many outlandish things happen in Olympia that it's hard to dismiss..."

"Then let me put your mind at ease about the matter. I, Josephine, hero of Athena and leader of the Warriors, swear upon my goddess and my life that I am telling the truth about everything and that the gods have toyed with the memories of their heroes, driven them to insanity, and then returned them to the mortal world as if nothing had happened. This do I swear."

Jasmin turned white as Josephine recited her oath. She straightened her back, rigid and distressed, and then grabbed Josephine by the arm. "You're coming with me to the Library, and you are showing me the documents you speak of this instant."

Josephine assented, trying to curb the smile creeping across her face. The two of them hurried out of the hotel.

Alexandria led the way up the stairs to the room. Her boots clattered against the uncarpeted wood and her hand trailed the worn and rusty railing. The whole hotel seemed to be falling apart: windows were cracked or taped so they would stay shut, the exposed wood belied its age, and the wallpaper was peeling off, forming small mounds of it on the floor. But it was cool and refreshing after having trekked in the hot Southern sun and it still smelled nice, like the whole place was inundated with eucalyptus and herbs.

She stopped at the room and knocked, as Brites came up behind her. They waited, and then Alexandria knocked again when there was no response. Still, not a sound emanated from the room. Brites looked askance at Alexandria, whose face contorted in fear and worry.

"Crap!" they exclaimed at the same time. Brites began shoving at the door, trying to open it through sheer willpower. Alexandria fumbled with her keys, pushing past Brites to jam them into the lock and shove the door forward, opening up the space.

They stepped inside.

"There's no one here," Alexandria said, surveying the bedrooms off the main room, all small with their doors half-opened. She took several steps forward and observed the living space. "They were– there's imprints in the chairs where they sat and that one's been moved from its spot."

"No signs of a struggle. It doesn't look like Josephine bested Jasmine and dragged her away," Brites added. "She must have taken her somewhere else. Do you think the Warriors found where they were?"

They passed from one room to the next; Alexandria's heart beat faster and faster as each one yielded no sign of Jasmin and Josephine. Nor were there signs of struggles. They looked through pillows and cushions and in closets, to make sure no weapons were sticking out and no people were hidden away; they searched for blood stains and proof of scuffling, but there was nothing. The whole place seemed completely undisturbed, as if no one had ever been there.

"This place would be swarming with them– or the room would show signs of being entered," Alexandria countered at last. "This looks more to me as if Jasmin was convinced to go to the Library by Josephine."

"Jasmin wouldn't do something that stupid..."

"She absolutely would," Alexandria disagreed, spinning around and staring at Brites. "Especially for the Library of Alexandria–"

Brites sighed, pressing her hand to her forehead. Worry

lines appeared on her face. "Josephine would be very persuasive, I'm sure. We have to go back to the Library and get them."

"We've already wasted half an hour, then, we've got to get going!"

Alexandria was already halfway out the door. She motioned for Brites to hurry up. They trekked down the stairs, past the lobby, and went back into the streets, forcing their way through the throngs of people back to the Library.

"And-" Alexandria said as they arrived at the dead-end street, "we still haven't seen Wen-Tang and Triniya. At what point do we start worrying that they're caught by the Warriors?"

"Maybe..." Brites said, opening the door. She stilled as the sounds of blades crashing carried through the bookshelves to them. "Right about now."

They ran in the direction of the noise, weapons already pulled. To their surprise, when they rounded the corner, it was not Warriors they found, but Egyptian priests at arms with the rest of the heroes. Josephine was trapped in the middle of Wen-Tang, Triniya, and Jasmin, who had backed themselves into a circle to fend off the Egyptians.

"What is the meaning of this?" Brite shouted over the clamour of fighting. Alexandria plunged straight into the mass of Egyptians, swinging her sword back and forth, being careful only to wound and not kill. They were not the enemy, though they needed to be stopped.

Asenath's head appeared from amongst the rabble. "Brites! We need your help– these Warriors are attempting to take over the Library!"

"These aren't Warriors, Asenath. They're heroes with me!"

Asenath's face turned white, and she blocked a blow from Jasmin before pulling on the Egyptian next to her. "These are not the enemy, stop fighting!"

The word soon spread and the whole fight came to a standstill. All that could be heard was heavy breathing and groans as people took stalk of their injuries and began to bandage them with ripped fabric from their tunics.

"We've been trying to tell you," Wen-Tang scowled at a man dressed in regal garments with an obscenely large turquoise ring, who gingerly pressed against his bleeding arm. "You should've listened."

He turned away from Wen-Tang and faced Brites.

"Welcome, Brites, friend of the Egyptians. Do you claim these people as your own?"

Brites looked at Josephine with a steady glance. "Yes, I do. If you don't mind letting them come with me, we have many things to do before the night is over."

He bowed his head. "The blessings of the House of Ra go with you then, daughter of Artemis."

Brites bowed in return and echoed the blessing. Then, she stalked towards Josephine, seized her arm and dragged her out. "Nice try," she hissed once they were out of earshot of the Egyptians. "You're lucky to be alive."

"I wasn't trying to escape," Josephine huffed. "I was showing Jasmin some documents stored here—"

"We didn't ask to be kidnapped by the Egyptians, either," Triniya cut in. "We were getting led out to be put on trial when we looped around a corner and saw Josephine and Jasmin rummaging through a bunch of scrolls. The Egyptians got distracted and then all of hell broke loose."

"It's a wonder you ran into us, actually," Jasmin said. "This place is massive."

Josephine snorted. "They keep their most precious documents the closest to their courts. It's really not a surprise at all."

"What documents were so important that you would risk bringing Josephine here, Jasmin?" Brites demanded. "We talked about this."

Jasmin swallowed, and it was only then the heroes realized that her face was rather pale. "Well, you see..."

"They're documents about what the gods do to heroes when they go mad," Josephine answered primly.

Wen-Tang, who followed behind them, stilled for a brief second, just long enough for Alexandria to bump into her.

"We need to keep go–" Alexandria started, but Wen-Tang clapped a hand over her mouth.

"Shh," she said. "Listen."

Brites eyed Wen-Tang, then Jasmin, and finally Josephine. "What the heck is this about?"

"Are none of you aware of this? That heroes go mad with the power of their gods and then are stripped of their memories and sent back to the mortal world? Surely, you must have been curious about what happened to your predecessors..." Josephine continued.

"Mine died protecting Olympia," Brites said tightly. "So no, I've never wondered about it. I was her lieutenant when it happened."

Josephine inclined her head. "I'm sorry. But my point still stands. Have you never wondered where heroes you were told stories about went? Why they never settled in Olympia to live the rest of their lives peacefully... why they seem to simply disappear from the records, never to be heard from again?"

"I guess not," Brites said slowly. "Most of them died in war."

"No." Josephine shook her head. "That's memories the gods have created." She pulled a scroll from inside her tunic and handed it to Brites once they were outside the Library. "Read it. You might find it enlightening."

Brites scowled at the scroll but opened it.

FROM THE ARCHIVES OF THE LIBRARY OF ALEXANDRIA

UNDATED | UNLISTED | AUTHOR UNKNOWN

These records have been written without the knowledge of the council of Olympians or the gods. It is enchanted so that they cannot find or read it. To any who have the fortune, or misfortune, of finding this parchment, be warned that it must be kept secret from the gods, or all of its knowledge will be lost.

I will not put my name in this parchment, for risk of being discovered. My work in Olympia must continue if I am eventually to rescue the heroes from their gruesome fates. For I have learned that the heroes of Olympia are fed the power of their gods so that they might properly serve them and command their followers. This divine essence weakens their mortal minds and begins, truly, to change their physical bodies. I have seen this on several, both living and deceased. The blood holds twinges of golden ichor and their skin is hotter to the touch. Their features begin to shift, so that they more closely resemble their god until they might be almost indistinguishable from them.

The god in question's power appears to act as a parasite on the hero's body, taking the form and turning the hero into a miniature of the god. If we lived in a world where gods perished, I would hypothesize that this was to ensure that the control of Olympia was always secured in "the gods," or their essences in human forms.

However, when the gods became immortal, this became a hindrance more than a useful trait. For they did not want the heroes to rebel against them or become too strong on their own. Instead, therefore, they began to wean the heroes from power. It caused the greatest tolls in the history of Olympia, though its records have been destroyed and the memories altered. Having found that the heroes needed their power in order to complete their duties, the gods then tried the reverse. They began to give the heroes more power, more than was necessary, but only as a reward for good service. They became dependent on the gods.

The mortals were overwhelmed with the influx and their bodies were unable to adapt fast enough to the changes. So, slowly, they began to go mad. Their minds were fragile and unstable and the slightest danger could destroy them. They began to die in droves, imploding on themselves. And the gods were once again faced with a dilemma: the heroes were dying late into their service, that was not the issue. It was that the other followers had begun to notice this trend and were scared of what it meant for them.

So, once more, the gods convened on Olympus to decide the fates of their servants. It was decided that when a hero began to show signs of madness, they would be taken to Olympus, where they would be stripped of their titles and powers, and their memories would be erased, and they would be sent back to the mortal world to live the rest of their days as normal humans once again. For this to work properly, the gods also erased from the history of Olympia any of the deceased heroes or their madness, and continued to erase it after each hero was sent away.

Those heroes never returned to Olympia, with two notable exception, one enacted by the goddess Ares, who succeeded in convincing the council to bring back Penthesilea in the days leading up to the destruction. She was the greatest of Ares' heroes and was sorely missed when command passed from her. The other exception was enacted by the king of the gods, Zeus, for his favourite hero, Atar. Atar had been driven the furthest to madness, for Lord Zeus' powers far outstrip those of his siblings. But he was brought back, his memories restored, and the gods crossed their fingers that he would not succumb to the darkness of his madness before he had completed his duty.

Alas he did, or so I saw as I stood on the battlefield and watched the destruction occur. Rather than helping the gods, he turned on them and killed them all, as if possessed, as if he were a new god come to take their place. He did not seem to think it was madness that drove him to these actions: no! He justified them to the other heroes when all was said and done, but they turned him away, sick with rage. Still, the heroes had no idea why he had done what he did.

I spoke to them afterwards and the consensus was simply that Atar had been plotting the downfall of the Olympians for years. They had no inkling of the storm underneath his skin. I did not inform them, for had they known, they would have become afraid and abandoned their posts. Olympia would have fallen into decay and died a long, painful death without its protectors.

Even now, having written this account, I do not think it wise to inform the heroes of the machinations of the gods. Some things are simply meant to remain secret and the heroes, when they are granted the privilege of their status, must take with it the dangers of the craft. I am not a hero, nor do I await the fate of the mad, but I have been here for many years and many have passed under my tutelage and watchful eyes.

Mortals are strange. Though many would turn down the position of hero with this knowledge, I am sure the worst of mortals would not. They are too greedy for power. Perhaps that is why the power of the gods corrupts them: they are so greedy for it that they lose themselves in it. Perhaps, they would forget why they were heroes in the first place. Perhaps the gods were right about what to do with them.

I am a mere scribe; I cannot pretend to hold the answers to the riddles of mortals and immortals. But my small amounts of knowledge have led me to this conclusion, and my wanderings over the centuries have led to the compilation of this short document. May it not pass into faulty hands.

CHAPTER 11
LONDON, THE UNITED KINGDOM

Day 9

Their trip to, and arrival in, London, was uneventful. Their plane landed at the scheduled hour, and they made it to the rooms they'd booked without any issues. None of them spoke about the scroll. Brites had shoved it back in her jacket after reading it and they did not bring it back out until they were safe in their hotel.

The view from outside the window was the only redeeming feature of the entire place: it featured the massive vista of church and temple domes, tall skyscrapers, and the vast complexes of the city skyline. None of was visible or noticed in that moment: everyone was far too tense and off-kilter.

"What are we supposed to do about this?" Jasmin asked, pointing at the scroll on the table. Wen-Tang was pacing back and forth on the other side. Brites leaned against the table, looking pale. Triniya rubbed Jasmin's shoulder comfortingly, and Josephine smiled from her chair with self-satisfaction.

Alexandria could see them all with perfect clarity from her perch.

"We can't just ignore this," Brites said, her voice shaky. Alexandria peered at her, watching how she was blinking back tears. "This is a breach of our rights as heroes and now that we have the hero council, we can do something about it."

"Not without letting the gods know that we found out," Wen-Tang snapped. "We can't give away how we got the information– they'd just wipe our memories and then we'd be right back to being clueless. We'd be truly doomed. Maybe there's some way to slow the process, give us more time– or even stop it?"

All eyes turned to Jasmin, who, as the Oracle of Delphi, had some training in medicine and herbs. She shrugged and cast her eyes back to the scroll. "It's beyond my ability to figure out. And the god of medicine hasn't returned to Olympia yet, so his whole realm is in disarray. Unless we wish to place our trust in Apollo and hope that he helps, I can't offer much. I am certain that the gods cannot do anything to us while we are of sound enough mind to refuse... but what happens when we lose our judgement ability, I am not sure."

"We could go back to the Library and see if there are any scrolls there that might have answers," Triniya suggested.

Brites immediately vetoed the suggestion. "We left because the Egyptians ordered us to. We can't impose upon them so soon after wreaking havoc there."

"Besides," Alexandria pointed out, nodding towards Josephine, "we still have a mission to complete. Athena isn't going to bide her time until we figure out a solution to our madness. Our priority should be stopping her, or we might not live long enough to go mad."

"Alexandria raises a good point," Wen-Tang agreed. "In its early stages, I doubt the madness is that dangerous. It likely creeps up on you, so that you almost don't notice it's happened at all. None of us noticed it in Penthesilea or Atar."

Brites hummed. "I always had a feeling that Atar was not completely sane. He was far too brash and god-like himself to be a normal human."

"You say that now." Wen-Tang rolled her eyes. "At the time, you were just as sure as everyone else that he was perfectly fine and the greatest leader the Olympian forces had ever had."

"It's beside the point," Jasmin interrupted. "Alexandria is right that we cannot abandon the quest. The temple of Mithras here in London has always been a safe haven for the Warriors. That has to be our priority– but we also cannot neglect this. We owe it to all of the heroes that will come after us and to those whose legacies we hold. And frankly, I don't know about you, but I don't like the idea of going insane."

"If I may interject..." Josephine stood up. Everyone stared at her, silently giving their assent for her to speak. "I've spent some time, during my off-hours, trying to find a solution to the issue. I have no wish to be mad either; in fact, I would very much rather not be driven to insanity. I haven't come up with a ton, but there is one solution I discovered when I was digging through the archives in Mithras' temple a couple of weeks ago..."

"What is it?" Wen-Tang asked quickly, leaning forward from her position. Alexandria watched the eagerness in her eyes and realized that Wen-Tang was fast losing control of herself, and was desperate, as much as she pretended to hide it, for a cure. She was running out of time. The other heroes were, too. *Even me*, Alexandria thought, *as new as I am, my countdown has also begun.*

"There's a plant that protects people from the trickery of immortals and from their powers. It's been used before successfully, and I thought it could be applied to this situation... but I can't remember where it grows. All I know is that by slowing the process down with the plant, we keep our minds sane enough that the gods aren't able to mess with them. The same way they can't enchant us? They can only wipe our memories if we are no longer functional. But that's all I know. I don't think I managed to get that far in the manuscript."

"Hang on," Brites jerked back. "How do we know we can trust you? You're our enemy, and you tried to escape in Egypt. It's not possible that giving us this information didn't serve some purpose for you... what are you trying to accomplish?"

Josephine bit her lip so that a line formed on her mouth. For several long seconds, she stared at Brites with her inscrutable gaze and Brites stared right back.

"I am unable to solve this issue on my own," Josephine finally relented. "I don't have the time, resources, or manpower to find a plant that may or may not keep me from going insane. Don't get me wrong. I still fully intend to help Athena take over Olympia and defeat you, but at this time, I'm willing to call a truce if you're willing to work with me. I can't return to my duties as Athena's hero knowing what is coming and knowing there's a chance I could change it. There wasn't anything I could do about it before, since I would have been on my own, but with all of us together..."

"How would you call a truce?" Jasmin said. "You can't tell Athena to back down so we can hunt an herb and then come back to fight her."

"No," Josephine admitted. "But I can forge a missive suggesting they push back the invasion a couple days due to the unrest in Olympia."

"Unrest?" came several cries from around the room. Alexandria lurched towards Josephine but did not touch her.

"What do you mean *unrest*?"

"Haven't you heard? Has no one in Olympia informed you?" Josephine's eyebrows crinkled. "Well, I certainly won't be the first. You're welcome to wait until your second in commands deign to inform you of their doings."

Wen-Tang wriggled in her chair. Everyone's heads turned towards her.

"I don't know anything," she said quickly. Alexandria frowned. *Too quickly.*

"What aren't you telling us?" Brites asked, a steely edge to her voice.

"Nothing!" Wen-Tang protested. "All right, well... not much, anyway. Zeus returned before I got back, but so did my sister... you remember Akira, right? The last thing I heard from her before joining the rest of you was that Zeus had picked his hero. A boy named Cernhelm... Atar's brother."

The silence was deafening.

"You're going to explain things right now." Brites stepped up towards Josephine and scowled. "Or so help me..."

"Well," Josephine shrugged. "If you insist... Olympia's at war with the North Guard. Atar has picked up one of your Amazons, Alexandria, as his second– a girl named Keilee, I believe– and is destroying the followings one by one."

Alexandria dropped her head into her hands in shock. The other heroes, in various positions around the dimly lit room, gasped and moaned, or stood up in fear and worry.

"How," Alexandria asked, shaking her head, "was I so stupid? Just to let Keilee off the hook? I should have known she'd somehow manage to almost rip Olympia apart."

Josephine crossed her arms and watched as the news sunk in for the heroes.

"It's not your fault," Jasmin replied soothingly. Her eyebrows furrowed and she pressed her hands together and then released them. "You had no way of knowing she'd do any of that. Besides, we're getting reports from her," she gestured towards Josephine. "It's hard to know how bad things actually are."

"I know," Brites sighed, rubbing her forehead with her finger. She leaned against the window and let her hair be pulled out the open entrance by the winds outside. "We have to trust that our people can control the situation. We can't fight two battles at once and right now, we need to focus on the situation here. It's developing far too quickly. We need to find a cure for the madness and then we need to stop Athena."

"Easier said than done," Wen-Tang scoffed. She tucked her hands into her pockets and scowled. "We sent our best people with North to assemble a following for Hermes and then we left, too. No wonder the North Guard chose now to attack us; Olympia was basically defenseless."

"You know Atar the best," Brites said. "How bad will it be?"

"If Keilee is helping to lead a force..." Wen-Tang began. She was interrupted by a pigeon landing on the windowsill. It cooed at them, not moving from its perch and watching them calmly, and Jasmin blinked, leaning forward to examine it.

"What the hell?" Wen-Tang demanded. "What's it doing?"

"I think it has a message!" Jasmin carefully picked up the pigeon and removed a roll of paper from a holder attached to its leg. She set the pigeon back on the windowsill and it fluttered away, its mission complete. In the confusion, none of the heroes noticed the small owl perched in the corner of the room, its wide eyes registering every movement. Jasmin's eyes widened as she unrolled the paper and skimmed the contents.

"What is it? Are we being tracked?" Alexandria asked, reaching for a weapon.

"No-" Brites said hurriedly. "It's a red pigeon. It's a message from the Amazons. They used to communicate with Artemis using those. They're the only red pigeons in the world, I think. The gods are reaching out to us, they have to be."

"Read the whole damn message, then," Wen-Tang ordered, taking a step forward. "Come on, Jas. What happened?"

"Don't call me that," Jasmin grumbled.

She held the letter up:

"To the Heroes of Olympia, from the Alliance,

Since the start of our war with the North Guard, none of our leaders besides Cernhelm have been lost since the death of Priya, Amazon. Command, therefore, remains in the hands of those appointed by you, with the exception of Tecmessa, selected by the Amazon council. Selena of the Hunters of Artemis had an encounter with a contingent led by Keilee the Amazon and one of Atar's people was captured, though the others, including Keilee, escaped. The future of Olympia remains uncertain for now. Talks have begun of an open-pitched battle.

The Alliance salutes you,

Cernhelm, Son of Justice, Ryn, first mate of the Twin Delphinus, Akira, Daughter of Aphrodite, Tecmessa, of the Amazons, Selena, Hunter of Artemis, Phoebe, Oracle of Apollo, Tarya, Vestal Virgin."

"Thank Chaos," Jasmin breathed once she finished reading. "They've got it under control. What a relief."

Josephine chuckled, but her reaction was ignored, except for Alexandria's harsh glare. *How dare she think this is all a joke.*

"Thank Chaos indeed," Alexandria said, making her best attempt to ignore Josephine. "But them not alerting us to an actual war being fought is unacceptable. When we get back, we'll need to handle the lack of communication." The others murmured their agreement.

Alexandria's heart pounded with the news, even as she forced a smile. *Priya is dead.* Who would lead the Amazons in her absence now? She fervently prayed that it was not

Hippolyta. *Priya is dead.* The thought rang in her mind like a deafening screech. *How can she be dead? How? How!*

She stood up and pressed her back against the wall, crossing her arms, trying to force the thoughts away. "We shouldn't delay our task. I'd like to get back to Olympia as soon as possible so I can reconvene with the Amazons. So, what's our plan?"

Wen-Tang rubbed the back of her neck and looked up at the ceiling. "We can assume Athena's here in London, given the star on the map just like the other places we've visited."

"The temple of Mithras is only a few minutes away," Triniya finally said from her corner of the room.

The owl, still hidden in the rafters in the ceiling, spread its wings and fluttered out the window. This time, everyone noticed it and jumped out of their seats in surprise.

"That answers our question of where we start!" Brites said. Altogether, they rushed out of the room and into the street. Triniya caught sight of the owl again and led the chase. They cut through the streets, cars swerving around them, but they didn't notice; they pursued the owl all the way to the steps of the temple of Mithras where it vanished into one of the windows.

"I guess we're starting right now," Jasmin announced.

CHAPTER 12
THE TEMPLE OF MITHRAS, LONDON

Day 9

It had been turned into a small museum, and when the girls tumbled into the front lobby, a perky young woman met them with pamphlets and informational cards at the ready.

"Is this your first visit with us?" she asked.

Jasmin shook her head. "No, thank you. We just wanted to look around again because we loved it so much. Do you mind if we just pop right in?"

The young girl seemed taken aback. "I'm sorry I didn't recognize you! Please, just make your way to the gallery and let me know if you have any questions."

Jasmin led the way to the elevators, and they all took it down to the bottom level. Everyone followed in silence as they passed through the galleries to the remnants of the actual temple, stuck behind a thin plastic partition. The doors closed behind them and an audio recording of Latin singing began playing over the speakers.

"It's just a hymn," Jasmin told Alexandria. "Not the original, but one they cobbled together from fragments. We want to-" Jasmin hopped the plastic barrier keeping the visitors from the stones in the center of the room. It was such a small museum that there wasn't even a security guard to protect the plastic barriers. The others followed suit and once they were all standing on the uneven, breaking rocks. Jasmin said, "There should be a way in from here, but I've never actually been in the underground complex. Any time I was here on business, it was before this was a museum and you could just walk in from upstairs."

"I know it." Josephine crossed her arms. She eyed them one by one, as if she were sizing them up for a fight before stepping forward into the center of the rocks and kneeling down to press into a small, innocuous red one that didn't match the other stones. Amidst the shuddering and stress of the stones shifting, an entryway appeared to their left: a staircase descending into a brightly illuminated space. The light carried from the bottom of the staircase to the top, inundating the usually dark temple room with glow.

"In we go!" Josephine said, leading the way. The others bounded after her, fearful she'd finally manage her escape, despite all of the oaths and promises she had made to help them. But she was waiting at the bottom of the stairs, a finger pressed to her mouth to warn them to be quiet. A gaggle of voices could be heard down the corridor, coming from behind a large wooden door.

"They're having a meeting," Josephine said. "Now is the best time to sneak into my room and grab that book. No one will dare question what I'm doing..."

"You sure Athena won't have informed them that you're a traitor?" Brites raised an eyebrow.

Josephine flushed. "It's fine. People are always coming and

going around here. Follow me." *I hope,* she thought to herself when they eagerly followed. *And if she does find us, then I need to think of a way to get us all out of here. Maybe the back entrance, if they haven't sealed it off yet.*

She led the way down the hallway, turning right before they reached the large doors that sealed off the meeting. Several twists and turns and numerous staircases later, they finally arrived at the residential quarters of the complex. There was a distinct difference in the very atmosphere of the two sections: all of the official corridors and rooms were gilded in gold and covered in tapestries, likely made by Athena herself, with large doors, spacious and open halls, and bright lights from above. The residences, on the other hand, were cramped and small, much darker and deeper underground. They were tucked away and separated from the ceremonial, as if they were an afterthought in the design of the complex and only the bare necessities had been added.

Even lights had been forgotten in the hallways and the whole place was barely illuminated by a handful of candles every couple of feet, precariously secured to the walls by previous Warriors who'd grown tired of groping their way at two in the morning. The ground, in contrast to the marble pavement from earlier, was packed dirt with the occasional cobblestone thrown in to differentiate it from the walls, which were the same packed dirt. It was less of a building and more of a tunneled system underneath the actual complex from whence, every morning, Warriors would emerge to begin their daily tasks.

"This one's mine when I'm here on a visit," Josephine said, finally pushing the door to one of the rooms open after they had walked down the long, depressing corridor for several minutes. It resembled the corridors in its bare, unfinished state. Josephine had clearly tried her best to make it as comfortable and homey as possible; what looked like handmade quilts and blankets were piled on the small bed and hung from the walls to hide the dirty brown. Lamps and candles were strewn over the bookshelves and desks to give the whole place a glow of warmth. Piles and piles of books were stacked against every possible surface, covered in papers, notebooks, and ink stains. A chest at the end of the bed held all of her clothing and necessities.

"Where did I put that book..." Josephine kneeled down and began rummaging through her various piles, pulling them out and leafing through them. Whether she was looking for specific information or simply reminiscing about having read those books, the other heroes could not tell. They stood around the room uncertain, tense, waiting as she went through several piles and scurried back and forth from desk to floor and floor to shelves in search of the precious tome.

Finally, when it seemed like all hope of ever locating the mysterious book had faded, she pulled one out from the bottom of the bookshelf, exclaiming, "Ah! This is it! I recognize the cover."

"Finally," Alexandria grumbled, leaning against the wall. "That took bloody forever."

"If we could hurry up," Brites scowled. "The longer we stand around, the more likely it is we'll caught. We know Athena is here."

"I'm sure we'll be fine," Triniya whispered. "Josephine said she was in a meeting."

"I don't trust Josephine as far as I can throw her," Wen-Tang argued back. "And if I had to put money on it, I'd bet Josephine is hoping Athena will show up. Athena knows we're here; we followed the owl after all. Twenty bucks, they're heading down the hallway right this second."

"The risk is worth it– you should know that better than

anyone, Wen-Tang, since you're losing your mind! And I've found the book now, anyway. I couldn't remember where I'd put it," Josephine said defensively. She flipped through it, stopping at a dog-eared page. "The plant's name is μῶλυ."

"Moly..." Jasmin whispered to herself. "Where do I know that from?"

Josephine laughed. "It's from the *Odyssey*, remember? I can't believe I didn't realize that earlier. It's the plant that Odysseus uses to protect himself from Circe's magic. It probably works against Olympian memory charms, as well."

"Circe!" Jasmin exclaimed. Brites smiled softly.

"She's lovely, when you're invited to the island," she whispered. "She's a great protector of nymphs..."

"It only grows there, though," Wen-Tang pointed out. "On her island. The Pirates have a task force that exists in the mortal world solely to protect that island from prying human eyes. It's almost impossible to get to and even if you manage it, the trip back is just as dangerous."

"I don't have any better ideas, though," Josephine pressed. "This herb, we know, works. A high enough dose of it should protect all of us. We don't have enough time to waste trying to think of another solution."

"Josephine's right," Brites said with reluctance. "We're not in a position to be picking our medicines. Wen-Tang, if you have Pirates guarding it, do you think they could drop us off and pick us back up?"

"I could command them to," Wen-Tang sighed. "As far as I know, they've never docked on that island before. We've always tried to keep a healthy distance when it comes to Circe and her plots. But given that the crew operates in the mortal world and I stay in Olympia most of the time, it's possible they *have* docked on the island and I just don't know about it."

"That's all well and good," Alexandria interrupted. "That we have a ride to the island, but how are we getting to the boat? Where is Circe's Island, anyway?"

"Out in the Pacific," Triniya answered. "That's where all the magical islands are."

"Triniya's right." Wen-Tang nodded. "The boat could pick us up in Alaska. That's where the refueling stations are for the ship."

"How the hell..." Brites began.

"Are we supposed to get to Alaska?" Alexandria finished.

A shuffle was heard outside the door. All of the heroes froze.

"Oh," a voice from behind them replied. They all spun around to be faced with Athena and a contingent of Warriors, smiling down upon them. "You're not going to Alaska. Instead, you'll be visiting my prison cells for a short period of time until we can have proper executions. You, too, you traitor," she shot at Josephine. "I'm surprised at how stupid and carelessly you acted, frankly. You followed me into the temple and thought you could slip by?"

"I-" Josephine floundered.

"We were actually hoping to run into you," Wen-Tang snarled. "We never finished our last fight. And you never gave us the information we wanted."

"I will strip you of your titles before this is all over and promote someone who is truly loyal to me," Athena continued speaking to her hero, as if Wen-Tang hadn't opened her mouth. "How dare you betray me to work for the enemy?"

"I didn't-" Josephine began but Brites interrupted her.

She tossed her dark black hair back as she stared Athena down. "We made her swear an oath."

Athena's glare focused upon Brites. "Warriors! Attack."

Her Warriors lunged into action and the small room erupted into chaos. Alexandria ducked to the side and hit a Warrior's head with the flat of her blade. Pressed into a corner, she furiously kept two others at bay, swinging from side to side almost wildly. Brites was the hardest-pressed, going one-on-one with Athena. She ducked and twisted and spun, only delaying the inevitable defeat that would come. Alexandria tried to get to her, to help fight off Athena, but the Warriors seemed to understand her goal and did everything in their power to keep her away.

A blood-curdling scream tore through the air. For a brief moment, all of the fighting paused as people turned to see where it came from: Wen-Tang, seemingly towering over the Warriors and the heroes, her eyes dark and stormy. She looked less like herself and more like Poseidon's child, with her black hair curling at the edges and the dark of her eyes spotted with the grey of a stormy ocean. She had grown a handful of inches. The crown of the Princess of Atlantis had appeared on her forehead and the twisting silver and gold and precious gems glimmered with some unknown light. She was regal– and she made Athena tremble.

"You should not be here," she told Wen-Tang, pushing Brites to the side, her grey eyes wide. "How have you evaded our watch for so long?"

"I don't know what you mean," Wen-Tang said. Even her voice sounded strangely far off and deeper. "I have evaded nothing."

Athena became aware of the other people watching her interaction and her lips tightened. "You must return to Olympia," she ordered. "For your safety and that of your people. Go see your patron– go see Poseidon."

"Why should I?" Wen-Tang challenged, stepping forward. Athena stepped back quickly.

"Do as I say. It is for all of our safety," Athena commanded, refusing to elaborate any further. Alexandria could see the glimmer of fear in her eyes. Whatever Wen-Tang was doing scared the Olympian; she guessed it was the madness finally settling into Wen-Tang's body, and that they were running out of time to find the moly plant. Alexandria strained her eyes, trying to read the minute expressions on Athena's face. She was scared, sure, but stolid. She did not speak. She did not attack the heroes again– *maybe Wen-Tang is more dangerous than we realize.*

"Warriors, exit," Athena declared. "The Olympian council will do far worse things to these heroes than we could ever hope to." And with that, Athena swept out of the room and the Warriors followed after her, fear and confusion on their faces.

Once they were gone, Wen-Tang seemed to shrink down to her usual size. Her hair straightened and her eyes became the clear brown that they normally were.

"What was that?" Jasmin asked, catching Wen-Tang's arm.

"I don't know-" Wen-Tang breathed heavily. "Whatever it is, I didn't do it on purpose."

"It's the madness," Alexandria and Josephine said at the same time. They looked at each other and then averted their gaze.

"Well, it worked," Triniya whispered. "We escaped Athena once again. She was terrified. Did you see her eyes?"

"She was remembering the destruction," Josephine muttered. "She had to be. We got lucky this time. Wen-Tang caught her off guard. She'll be prepared to deal with a mad hero next time– and she'll find a way to warn the other gods despite the coming war between them; they'll come after us and they won't be happy. We've got to get to Circe's Island as fast as we can, before Athena has a chance to tell them. She's right– they'll do far worse things to us than she could. Follow me, we're taking the back way out. If they haven't sealed it off."

Alexandria fell behind with Wen-Tang as they went down the rest of the hallway, dank and dark, until they reached a staircase that let out in the middle of a London underground system. They hadn't been lucky about many things this mission, but at least they were lucky about this.

"What did it feel like?" Alexandria whispered, not necessarily wanting the other heroes to overhear her.

The Pirate shrugged. "Honestly, it felt good. It felt like a release of all of the anger and energy I've had since we started this quest. I don't know how I did or if I can control it, but I kind of want it to happen again. It made me powerful."

"You terrified Athena."

"I know." Wen-Tang's eyes glinted with pride as she looked at Alexandria. "It was amazing to know I have that kind of power. For once, I felt like the gods couldn't tell me what to do or control me. If this is what the madness is like, I don't want to get rid of it."

"I don't think the moly gets rid of it," Alexandria mused. "Not based on anything Josephine's told us, at least. It probably just lessens the effects. And protects us from the gods. But maybe I'm wrong."

"The gods couldn't touch me anymore," Wen-Tang shook her head. "I could beat them. I know I could."

"You sound very sure about that."

"I can feel the power, even now. It's like it's dormant in my blood and will wake up when I need it to defend myself. I understand why Atar killed all the gods during the destruction now... I shouldn't have judged him for those actions so hard. Maybe he was right. Maybe the gods do have to go..."

"Wen-Tang!" Alexandria hissed, grabbing her arm and squeezing. "You can't say things like that. You swore an oath to serve Poseidon and to protect Atlantis."

Wen-Tang blinked several times and then deflated. "I know," she mumbled finally. Her entire body seemed slumped over, as if she were both exhausted and broken– her head hung limply and her feet shuffled, too heavy to be picked up. "I know I did. I'm just high on the feeling; don't take anything I'm saying seriously. I know my duty. I know we need to fix this before it gets worse and I can't control it."

"We'll figure it all out somehow," Alexandria assured her. They had no choice but to.

They passed through the tunnels of the underground and changed tubes several times to get back to their hotel just as the evening sky died into its dark night.

INTERLUDE
A COMMON SPACE, LONDON HOTEL ROOM

Day 9

"How are you feeling?" Jasmin asked, handing Wen-Tang a cup of tea and cradling her own in her hands. "Is it exhausting?"

The room was less dingy than their previous hotels. In fact, it was almost nice, with its faded flower wallpaper and its old but clean carpets that were worn where furniture used to be. The kitchen was small and cramped and completely covered in wood and marble, but it was functional and had a charm of its own. It came to life in the late night once the lights were dimmed and the curtains to the porch had been shut to keep the bugs out.

"A little bit," Wen-Tang said, taking a gulp of the drink. "But it feels good more than anything else. I don't feel as stressed or worried as I have been since we left Olympia."

"A release." Jasmin nodded in understanding. "I've never seen something like that– and honestly, it was just in the nick of time. I really didn't believe we'd manage to get out of there alive."

"Neither did I," Wen-Tang agreed. She stretched out from her curled-up position and stood, pacing the room with her cup of tea up at her mouth. "But the idea of losing to Athena after working so hard to stop her seemed so ignoble and stupid that I couldn't stand it."

"What I don't understand," Jasmin stood up and faced Wen-Tang, "is why this is afflicting you already. I've been a hero much longer than you– and so has Triniya. But neither of us are exhibiting any of your traits, and I don't feel like I'm going mad."

"I think," Wen-Tang said with a measured tone, "it has to do with taking on the crown of Atlantis. My patron god is just more powerful than yours or Triniya's because it's Poseidon, but I'm also a part of the royal family of Atlantis now. When I live there, I'm inundated with his power and magic the entire time, with no reprieve."

"Extra privileges," Jasmin nodded. "Means extra power."

"Precisely. But you're sure that you don't feel any of this? You don't feel constantly angry or worried? Like everything is bubbling under your skin, just waiting to be let loose? Because Alexandria says she's had a similar feeling and she's the newest of us all, except for Josephine. And Ares isn't that much stronger than Apollo or Hestia."

"I'm sure some of us just have a higher tolerance for power," Jasmin mused. "Whether it's because of a bloodline or simply luck, we aren't as affected. And remember, Alexandria had the whole debacle with the sword of Penthesilea. She was probably being exposed to more of Ares' raw power than normal."

"I suppose that makes sense," Wen-Tang agreed. "You should get some sleep though, Jasmin. Thank you for staying up with me but I'm okay, I promise."

"Are you sure?"

"Mhmm."

Jasmin took one final, long sip of her tea and placed it on the marble countertop. She nodded to Wen-Tang and passed by her to one of the rooms with an open door. "Let me know if you need anything, okay?"

"I will."

The door shut and Wen-Tang stood alone in the common room. She looked around for a second, took a sip of her drink, and sat down on the couch again. It was lonely at this hour of the night, even when she knew that everyone was in their rooms, sleeping, recovering for the trip to Alaska in the morning. She wished Alexandria would wake up and talk to her. For all of Jasmin's comforting aura, she understood nothing of what was happening in Wen-Tang's mind. And Alexandria did.

But no door cracked open and no footsteps drew near, so Wen-Tang sat there on the couch until the early hours of the morning, when she finally managed to doze off until the first trickling in of early risers appeared to make breakfast.

CHAPTER 13
ALASKA, THE UNITED STATES

Day 12

Winter had bitten into Alexandria's skin with its harsh freeze and irate winds. She burrowed her face into her coat, but it did nothing against the stinging of the winter air that she could still feel like a phantom on her cheeks, despite being inside. It was hopeless. She was already in a foul mood. The plane trips had been plagued with several delays and a missed connection, and they were several hours behind schedule. And now, Wen-Tang was trying to find their ship, so they were all waiting in a small, fish-smelling inn until she returned. A bowl of stew had been placed before her, but Alexandria couldn't find it in herself to take her hands out of her pockets, where they were warm, even though she was starving.

Somehow, no one else seemed to be struggling with the cold like she was. The other heroes appeared at ease as they ate their stew and bread and chatted about various small matters from their lives as mortals. Jasmin and Josephine appeared to have become close and were comparing notes on various books that Alexandria had never heard of. Brites and Triniya had found common ground in discussing some technicalities of a festival in Olympia that they needed to start planning once everything with Athena was handled.

Alexandria sat there and watched them, feeling completely separated from the scene. None of them tried to pull her into the conversation or ask her opinion; they seemed to have all silently agreed not to speak to her. Alexandria wondered if part of it had to do with the sour expression on her face. But then again, Wen-Tang now constantly looked as if she were on the edge of murdering someone and that didn't seem to be an issue.

The door burst open, and within the flurry of snow and wind a person emerged, shutting the door behind her. Wen-Tang pulled her cowl off her face, revealing the warm, pink skin, so heavily contrasted with the white ice sticking to her eyelashes and hair. Her eyes roamed the inn until they landed on the other heroes, and she walked towards them, settling into the spot next to Alexandria on the bench.

Before she spoke, she tore a large piece of bread off and stuffed it in her mouth. When she'd chewed and swallowed, she said, "They're preparing the boat now. We have about half an hour to get on board. It's a ten-minute walk, but it's snowing heavily, so the sooner we leave, the better. We don't want to get caught in the ice here."

"We've already been delayed long enough," Alexandria scowled. "The gods know that."

"I think the gods know all too well," Wen-Tang agreed. "This weather isn't normal for this time of season. I've heard some locals complain about it. If I had to guess, Athena made the others aware of what's happened to me in some roundabout way, and we're being pursued. I'd hoped we'd have more time."

Brites stood up. "Then it's in our best interests to leave immediately."

Triniya grabbed another bread roll before she stood up, and the others followed suit: taking one last sip of their warm drinks, swallowing one last spoonful of their stews, or stuffing a bread roll into their pockets to enjoy on the ship. Alexandria was the only one to not touch any of it; she couldn't muster the energy to eat when every small thing the others did set her off or when it was so blasted cold.

The trek to the boat, led by Wen-Tang, was as miserable as Alexandria had anticipated it would be. She refused to look up and trudged wearily in the snow, kicking at it with the edge of her boots. The warmth of the inn – though she hadn't properly appreciated it at the time – seemed like a dream compared to the cold outside. It seemed especially cruel that they would have to brave the outdoors and then the open sea in the middle of what was becoming a blizzard.

Snow swirled around them, swallowing them in its iciness. Josephine fell behind and matched pace with Alexandria, her head turned down to look at her boots and protect her face from the gnawing winds. Her soft blonde hair was coated in droplets of ice, tangled and knotted. Alexandria hazarded a glance towards her, unreciprocated. Josephine's entire body was rigid, as if she were either trying to stop shivering or as if she were bracing herself for a fight. Both were equally as likely, Alexandria thought, if the gods were pursuing them.

She didn't imagine Ares would have much to do with it. The goddess had seemed perfectly fine with driving Alexandria to semi-madness with the sword of Penthesilea. *No*, Alexandria thought, *that's probably why I feel as if I am going mad, so soon after becoming a hero. It's not fair. Jasmin and Triniya have done this so much longer than I have and seem absolutely fine.*

"You seem worried," Josephine finally said, in the interlude between two waves of the wind. It was so loud that unless there was a lull, you couldn't hear someone beside you shout, just the constant roaring of air.

"I'm not talking to you about it!"

"You think you're going mad," Josephine continued. "I've watched you since you caught me on that beach-" she grimaced at the word *beach*, as if realizing again that they were stuck in an endless winter now. "I didn't know you beforehand, so I can't be sure what you were like, but I don't think these are the symptoms of madness. They're certainly not the same ones Wen-Tang is experiencing."

"I *said* I'm not talking to you about it."

"You don't have to!" Josephine retorted. "I'm just saying! Wen-Tang is undergoing a physical change–if you're dealing with anything, it's simply adjusting to being a hero. I'm going through the same thing, you know– maybe we could..."

Alexandria stopped, spun around, and blocked Josephine from walking. "We're not going to become friends, Josephine. The others may trust you after Athena threatened to kill you and you offered to help them find the moly, but I don't. I won't be that easily won over. I dealt with betrayal in my ranks as soon as I became Ares' hero and I'll be damned if I get fooled again by you."

"Jasmin mentioned something about that– a war between the Amazons and the Hunters." Jasmin seemed to seize upon the chance to talk to Alexandria, but the other hero shook her head and continued walking, catching up to the group and leaving Josephine behind in the snow.

They had trekked down the length of the main town street and onto the docks, and the looming masts and riggings of their ship sprawled in the ocean before them. It was alive with commotion as sailors bundled heavily in scarves, hats, and gloves, tried to prepare her to take off.

As Wen-Tang led the party on board, a young man appeared in front of them, bowing lowly to Wen-Tang.

"This is Captain Hendrick," Wen-Tang announced. "He's been in charge of guarding Circe's Island since right after I became Poseidon's hero. He knows this area better than anyone else."

"It's nice to meet you all," Hendrick shouted at them, to be heard over the wind. Alexandria picked up the faintest hint of an accent which she couldn't place. "I come from Norway, where the seas are much rougher and colder than this. You do not need to worry about reaching your destination safely. This ship has weathered many a terrible storm and will do so once again. But I can see that you are cold. Please, join me in the captain's lounge for some warm refreshments and a nice fire. My men will have us setting off shortly." His voice was scratchy by the end of his long shout.

"That would be a relief," Jasmin screamed back. The others all nodded enthusiastically, except for Wen-Tang who slipped off to speak to the rest of the crew, while Hendrick led the heroes to the lounge. Stepping in, they were hit with the tingling sensation of ice melting off of their faces and the nerves in their hands and feet slowly warming again. It was almost unbearably painful, and Alexandria grimaced as she shook snow onto the carpet and took off her coat. She settled herself right next to the fire and raised her hands to feel the flames. As unpleasant as the melting sensation in her bones was, it felt nice not to be cold.

Relief washed over her body. The tingling sensation faded and all she felt was the deep, satisfying warmth settling into her. Finally, she tuned in to the conversation around her, which was already in full swing.

"If all goes according to plan," Hendrick explained, "we should be there by tomorrow evening. If nothing goes according to plan, then we'll see– the gods can be very nasty when it comes to the high seas. Fortunately, you'll have the favour of Poseidon, since we're carrying the Princess of Atlantis. The ocean itself will not betray us."

Alexandria narrowed her eyes. That seemed too fortunate.

Their mission had been disaster after disaster, as far as she was concerned, and there was simply no way this would be easy. Especially not with the threat of the gods pursuing Wen-Tang. *I wonder if the storm has anything to do with it.*

A loud horn blew, resounding through the entire ship.

"Sounds like we're taking off," Hendrick announced, and the ship rocked forward, slowly pushing itself away from the docks and into the coming storm. From the windows outside the cabin, Alexandria could see the flurries as they swirled past or stuck themselves to the cold ice. She wondered if it would be possible to get her tongue stuck on the inside of the glass, like when she'd licked a metal pole her first, and only, visit to Canada as a young girl.

The winds picked up. Waves hit against the side of the ship, their noise drowning out the shuffling of feet on the boat. Alexandria leaned back in her chair in the cabin, trying to warm herself by hugging her chest. Hopefully, Circe's Island was warmer than this bloody weather.

CHAPTER 14

SCYLLA AND CHARYBDIS, THE ARCTIC OCEAN

Day 14

"I've never seen the ocean this angry," Wen-Tang said. Hendrick raised his eyes to the sky.

"Neither have I, and I've sailed these waters for a long time. The gods must truly be irate with someone."

Wen-Tang pursed her lips. She couldn't tell Hendrick that it was her fault that they were being pursued by this horrible storm. The water tossed the ship to and fro like it was a toy; the winds howled and whirled too much for them to put up the sails and steer in any direction. They were completely at the mercy of the gales, and those gales were leading them straight to the pass between Scylla and Charibdis, behind which lay Circe's Island. Still, they moved quickly. Two days into their travels, and Wen-Tang already calculated that they'd gone at least four hundred nautical miles, with the wind blowing them further out to sea every passing second.

"At least we're going in the right direction– and fast," Wen-

Tang pointed out. Her hat threatened to fly off her head, but she caught it in one hand and clutched it to her chest.

Hendrick shook his head. "Not as good as it sounds. Unless I can control every minute movement of this ship, we're likely to run into the monster or the whirlpool. I've done this pass several times with success, but it is never easy. I do not trust," he paused, as if unwilling to admit to the reality, "that we will survive this time." His eyes shifted back and forth, nervous. "I don't know what's happening. But something's wrong. The winds are moving us too fast for me to have enough say in our course, and the waters are so churned from this storm, I fear they will throw us off-kilter at a crucial moment. Poseidon never lets this happen to us, and we have you, a royal of Atlantis, on board... something is very wrong. Perhaps Poseidon has lost control of his own domain– no, what am I saying, that's impossible. I'm sure it's nothing."

Wen-Tang grimaced, her heart pounding faster in her chest. "Are you scared?"

The captain considered for a moment. "No. I have accepted my fate. I have lived long past my prime. But a captain goes down with his ship," Hendrick declared. "And I intend to fulfill the role you gave to me with all of the strength I have in my body."

A captain goes down with the ship. Wen-Tang hadn't forgotten the wise words, and in her own life, had tried her best to exemplify them. She'd always been the first to lead a charge and the last to leave danger. *But I'm refusing to go down with my ship now. I brought this storm upon us and here I am, standing on the deck, pretending it's not my fault. If I left Hendrick and the others, the storm would follow me. I could survive it on my own. Or, if it comes down to it, I will face the gods in combat.* The longer the thoughts passed through her mind, the more inspired Wen-Tang became. *I will be like one of the heroes of old. I will live and die with glory and honour in my actions, even if I am the only one who knows it.*

"I must see to something in the hold," Wen-Tang said, interrupting Hendrick's further remarks upon the fine points of navigating between two terrible fates. She surprised herself with the abruptness of her decision; she couldn't remember choosing to speak. "If you'll excuse me."

She did not wait to hear his farewell before she set out down the stairs and into the hold to find provisions for herself and a warmer coat. Her hands trembled as she picked the coat up, but her mind did not waver in its decision. *A captain goes down with the ship.* She rummaged in the kitchen and found a couple packs of hard tack. There was no other choice. As she rummaged for a pair of gloves in the storage room, she tried to think of counter-arguments to her decision, but her mind was so hazy, and yet so focused, that none came. *It must be the right decision, then,* she thought to herself. *It's the only way I can make sure the mission succeeds.* Once she'd found everything she needed, she ascended back onto the deck and blended into the busy crowds of sailors doing their best to keep the ship together against the fracturing ice and wind. She dropped her haul into one of the lifeboats and climbed in, slowly lowering herself.

Every move she made seemed to be involuntary. It did not feel like she was in control of her body anymore; it acted without her authority. As much as part of her mind willed her to stay on the boat and find the moly, to protect herself against the gods, the other part, the part she knew was correct screamed and fought and won. Wen-Tang's hands shook as they untied the ropes and unfastened the paddle. Her entire body trembled and goosebumps appeared on her arms. *I don't want to do this, I don't want to do this, I don't want to do this,* she told herself. And she did anyway, incapable of halting. It was as if her mind was controlling her body, but Wen-Tang was no longer in her mind. Briefly, she thought, *The madness.*

The boat splashed into the water and cold droplets landed on the sleeves of her jacket. Wen-Tang repressed a shiver and picked up her paddle. Slowly and methodically, she pushed herself away from the boat, fighting against the winds and the storm as she guided the small boat into a running current, which quickly swept her away from the sailing ship, and in the opposite direction. She couldn't stop; she felt compelled to continue.

Just as she expected, the storm followed her, dragging itself over the ship and engulfing her in its icy tentacles. When she craned her neck behind, she could see the blue skies ahead for Hendrick's ship and the other heroes.

A captain goes down with her ship, Wen-Tang reminded herself, picking up her paddle again. It did very little to move the boat in any direction, but the motion kept her warm as the cold seemed to chill her very core. She closed her eyes– there was no point in keeping them open, since she couldn't see where she was going– and tried to summon the strength she'd felt in that moment of madness, but it escaped her. Above the howling wind, she heard a crack. The lifeboat shuddered and Wen-Tang looked down in panic to see a massive hole in the ship. The cold had eaten away at the wood and now her boat was sinking under the weight of the water filling it. She tried to stand, pained by her soaking pants, but her frenzied movement sent everything tipping, and she fell into the great blue depths.

It was silent. It was still. And, Wen-Tang thought, it was strangely calming. The cold no longer made her uncomfortable. She felt like she was floating in an endless vacuum of quiet and stillness. Her limbs no longer cooperated, and her breathing no longer worked. But it did not matter. She was the princess of Atlantis. She could survive underwater indefinitely, suspended in this strange, inanimate moment. Time and space and the whole world melted away. She almost forgot who she was herself, and it was liberating.

What did it all matter? The gods? Olympia? Her position as a hero and a princess and a member of a council? All of it faded away when you considered fate and the end of all things. None of it lasted. Her life was the merest blip in a long, drawn-out story of existence and whether she lived or died now would not change things in the end.

Wen-Tang felt the darkness of madness descend upon her, as if it were trying to protect her from the cold that had made its way to the roots of her soul.

Dusk rolled in, with its brilliant hues of orange and yellow, red and pink, that lit up the sky. The clouds dissipated into the horizon, captured the colours in their mists and held them there, like a painting of a sunset, frozen in time. Alexandria, pacing the deck, was lost in thought. Every now and again, her eyes darted to the ocean and watched the waves beat against the hull of the ship rhythmically, much gentler than they had been hours ago. The storm seemed to have dissipated over the course of the day; she breathed a sigh of relief at the thought.

The quiet suddenly shattered. Alexandria startled as the cries began to spread throughout the ship.

"Has anyone seen Wen-Tang?"

"Wen-Tang!"

"Where did she go?"

"She's missing?" Alexandria shouted, in answer to the calls. Her heart sped up, pounding in her ears. *How do you lose someone at sea?* she thought. Panic climbed into her throat.

The ship resounded with the calls of the heroes as they searched for Wen-Tang amongst the ropes and barrels. But still, no sign of the Captain appeared. Alexandria darted to and fro, her eyes flitting nervously, straining and trying to find the telltale straight, jet-black hair. She clambered behind boxes and rummaged through barrels. She burst into every room she could find, hoping Wen-Tang had simply fallen asleep somewhere.

Her bundles of warm clothing were finally shed now that the storm had passed. It was as if the weather was insane: one second, cold and freezing, it felt as if they were all about to perish. The next, warm and sunny, like they'd entered into a tropical paradise. She had stripped to her t-shirt but still felt comfortable underneath the sharp sun. It was as if she were at home, in Mexico, except on a boat instead of in the mountains with her sister.

Triniya ran around, shuffling through large boxes and barrels, more and more desperate by the moment. Brites helped her flip boxes and rummage through hidden corners frantically. Jasmin stood at the helm, almost paralyzed with worry for the hero. Alexandria could vaguely see the fear in her eyes, sparkling and bright.

Minutes ticked away, feeling like they were hours, and still there was no sign of the pirate. They continued to search, their hearts dropping more and more with each minute.

Alexandria caught Josephine's eye. The other girl smiled softly. As if she had expected Wen-Tang to do something. Or perhaps it was one of pity; Alexandria could no longer tell. Jasmin's eyes were watery, but she did not begin to cry. Alexandria thought she might lose her mind. *Am I seeing things? Does Josephine know something?*

"One of the lifeboats is missing!" Hendrick shouted. Alexandria rushed over towards him with the rest of the heroes, who consolidated around the railing and looked down. Sure enough, one of several lifeboats was missing and its ropes dragged in the water. Alexandria leaned over and tried to peer into the horizon, but if Wen-Tang really had taken off, the storm was obscuring her. It was far behind them, hiding the whole of the coast.

"She took the storm with her," Alexandria whispered. "She tried to save all of us." Her heart sank and her stomach churned at the idea. *She's really gone completely mad.*

"What did Captain Wen-Tang do that angered the gods so much?" Hendrick asked. "If you don't mind me prying, that is. I've never seen such a storm in all my life, and I'd be right curious to know what caused it."

Jasmin exchanged glances with Alexandria and shook her head. All of the heroes remained silent, and Hendrick waited patiently for an answer. Finally, Brites spoke up, her voice trembling. Her eyes were vacant and glazed over, and she appeared completely disassociated. "It has to do with our mission, Hendrick. Unfortunately, until it's over, we can't disclose any of it without putting you and your crew in danger."

"Is that why you have to get to Circe's Island?"

Brites nodded.

"Well, we'll be there shortly enough– d'you think we could maybe find the Captain and help her afterwards?"

"I don't know," Brites answered, choking on her own voice. "I don't think so. I think we have to let her–" she fell silent. Her lip trembled. The memories came flooding back to Alexandria, of Brites cradling Sophia's dead body.

"Oh, Capt'..." Hendrick sighed. "Oh, Capt'."

"She's strong," Jasmin said quietly. "She'll be okay- I'm sure she will."

No one believed her. Everyone stood there in contemplation, watching the rippling of the waves as they struck the boat and were shifted to the side. Triniya dropped her head down to her chest and let out a sob; then, she rubbed her sleeve over her eyes and straightened her back again. Alexandria nodded at her approvingly. *We need to control ourselves. There's still a mission to finish. Maybe we can find Wen-Tang and save her if we get the moly.*

"She was a good captain." Hendrick broke the deafening silence. "A right good one. She found me this position after my brother died in Poseidon's temple and I couldn't stand living in Olympia anymore. Couldn't stand leaving either..."

Brites hummed in acknowledgement, sounding mournful.

"Don't let my old yarns keep you. I'm sure you're anxious to find some way to reach Wen-Tang. I'll leave you to it and get up on the wheel– I have– the route is rough, from here– if you manage to send her a message, tell her the crew was glad of the visit."

"We will," Jasmin promised. Hendrick pushed through them and headed up the stairs to the helm station. As he passed by Alexandria, she saw the glimmer of a tear in his eye. For some reason, that small tear pained her more than anyone else's reactions. Wen-Tang's disappearance– *and possible death,* Alexandria thought to herself, *in that storm*– disturbed him, as much as he pretended to be nonchalant about it.

It disturbed *her*. She wondered why Wen-Tang had decided to do it. *Was it the madness that took over? Are the gods controlling her mind?* If the storm had been sent because of her, then it would not release her. She would sink in that little lifeboat and the cold waters of Alaska would swallow her whole.

Time seemed to freeze.

CHAPTER 15
SCYLLA AND CHARYBDIS

Day 14

"Scylla and Charybdis coming up!" the lookout shouted. "All hands on deck!"

Alexandria suddenly felt weak; she pressed her back against the railing and sank to the ground. She couldn't remember what she'd done for the past hour, lost in a haze of grief over Wen-Tang, but the deck was alive around her as they neared the monsters.

She had spent so little time as a hero and yet already, she felt as if daggers were being jammed into her chest. People were dying all around her. Maybe that was what drove the heroes mad and not the power of the gods. Just the constant losing of people you loved, or liked, or knew.

"Lean to the right!" Hendrick shouted. She heard the catch in his breath. The crew burst into action, ignoring the pained tone of their captain. She looked up at him and felt a pang in her chest, something she couldn't quite name. A kind of admiration and respect that despite his emotions, despite his grief, despite his fear, he was carrying through with his mission anyway.

"Leant to the left!" he shouted again.

She craned her head to stare out at the water from between the rail posts and saw the massive underbody of Scylla rearing upwards as its heads tried to reach the ship. It was hulking and horrifying: with water dripping down its massive body, it looked like one of the monsters Alexandria dreamed of in her nightmares. Large barrels of meat fell into the water in front of her. The heads dove for them, and she caught a glimpse of the reptilian monstrosities, with their bulging yellow eyes and sharp bright teeth, rotted black. Its nostrils flared, with streams of seawater pouring from them. Every move it made was wild and unpredictable as it thrashed in the sea, as if it were struggling to hold itself up. In one of its mouths, it held a piece of old carrion from the barrels. Alexandria pinched her nose shut with her fingers as the smell wafted over her: dead meat and ancient sea monster, decaying before her very eyes, but also still very alive.

The horror locked eyes with Alexandria and she shuddered. It seemed as if it could read her mind. It leaned forward, as if it were considering dropping the carrion and taking her instead. Its long, scaly neck twisted and turned, as if it was preparing to make a kill strike. But it rose back to join the rest of the heads, munching on its trophy. Her heart beat out of her chest, and her skin felt clammy and sweaty.

Even from her side of the deck, she could see the swirling waters of Charybdis spraying onto the sailors manning the ropes. Several of them lost their grip and went flying into the cabins and the food stockpiles. They overturned barrels, and pounds of oranges came flying through the railing, tripping others. They plopped into the ocean, sinking down, only to reemerge like small cannonballs aimed at the sails when Scylla splashed the waters, searching for prey. One or two sailors fell overboard into the lifeboats or into the water, Alexandria couldn't be sure. She could make out the distinct clothing of the other heroes: Jasmin's yellow top was on the helm deck, next to Hendrick; Brites and Triniya held onto each other, pressed against a stack of boxes that seemed to be stabilizing them; Josephine appeared right at home, helping the sailors move the ship on the demanding angles that Hendrick required.

Alexandria turned back to look at the monster. *We're all going to die. There's no way we can get out of this.*

Scylla finished her carrion, and its several heads lunged for more food. Alexandria ducked, expecting to be picked up and chomped down on. *I'm not ready to die!* The rancid breath of the monster covered her; she gagged. Shutting her eyes tight, Alexandria tried to pretend that Scylla wasn't there, but she could almost feel every move the slimy, snake-like necks made, as if every nerve in her body was completely on edge. But the expected blow, the teeth sinking into her, the fear and the realization, and the moment of death, never came. She slowly opened her eyes.

More barrels of carrion were thrown overboard. Scylla turned away from her live prey to hunt for the easier, dead meat.

Hendrick ordered the sailors to full speed and the ship flew by the two dangers. *Hendrick saved us all,* Alexandria thought. *He saved me from Scylla.* She closed her eyes and breathed in deeply, and suddenly, the seas were calm.

CHAPTER 16
CIRCE'S ISLAND

Day 15

The waters and the sky were silent. Circe's Island was visible on the horizon with its calm little inlet and small dock, its swaying palm trees and bright white beaches. Alexandria watched dolphins zip by the side of the boat and dance amidst the waves as if they had not a care in the world. After the harrowing crossing to the island and after the week spent crisscrossing the length of Europe on what appeared to be a futile quest, Alexandria felt relief that peace had finally prevailed.

Perhaps we've reached the end of the difficulties, she thought to herself, though she knew well that there was much more still to come. They had to get the moly plants and then they still had to deal with Athena. *Though, if Josephine feels so betrayed by Athena, maybe she'll willingly give her testimony to the Olympian council. And then we can go home and rest until the next misadventure occurs.*

Going home so they could be safe and not lose any more friends sounded like a luxury.

"All hands on deck!" Hendrick shouted. Out came sailors pouring from every direction onto the forecastle. They surrounded Hendrick and cheered as he announced they had safely re-entered the waters of Circe's Island. Others remained at their posts, working more quietly and slowly so they could also hear the announcements. Alexandria stood up and joined the crowd. She pressed in on them and they parted through to let her to the front, where she joined the other heroes. As Hendrick thanked his men for their bravery, she felt a stab of guilt that they'd ever asked him to brave Scylla and Charybdis again. Still, it had to be done.

She looked up at him. His face seemed to have morphed from when they'd shook hands at the port in Alaska. No longer did he look like a boy in a costume, swaggering about as the captain of a ship that spent its time sailing around a peaceful island. Now, Alexandria saw the regal bend of his brow and the sharpness of his blue eyes as they met hers and then looked at the crowd of people under his control. His blonde hair was blown to the side and soaked, but it curled on his temple and around his ear. The cap on his head shone underneath the bright sun. Alexandria found it impossible to stop looking at him; she could barely concentrate on his words, which for the most part didn't seem to be addressed to her anyway.

No. It's a stupid crush. I don't have time for that, she scolded herself. *Forget about it, Alexandria. You've got too much to do.*

"We'll be dropping our heroes on the docks tomorrow morning," Hendrick announced. "And you will all have the day off to spend as you please on the beach– so long as you remain respectful of the Lady Circe's property. I don't want to have to rescue any of you this time!"

Everyone laughed. Two sailors behind Alexandria leaned

forward and explained to the heroes that last time they had spent a day on the island, a few of the men had gotten hungry and picked fruit from Circe's gardens. As punishment, they were turned into pigs. Alexandria laughed politely, but her attention was still entirely focused on Hendrick. His cheeks were pink as he tried to hold in his laughter. She continued berating herself internally.

"Settle down, settle down!" he ordered. The noise immediately ceased. "As I said, you'll all have the day off. Onshore at seven in the morning sharp, onboard at seven in the evening sharp! That goes for you all as well, heroes– we don't sleep on the island if we can help it. There are too many snares and enchantments for us mortals to be safe. We'll spend the night on the dock and then leave in the morning for Alaska again, to drop the heroes off. After that, it'll be operations as normal for us. And while I still have you all here and your undivided attention– which is very hard to come by– a couple announcements for the upcoming month!"

One loud groan echoed throughout the entire assembly, and then everyone was silent again. Alexandria blushed when Hendrick looked down at her; she averted her gaze, embarrassed, and quipped at Jasmin that she felt like one of the crew all of a sudden.

"I can see why Wen-Tang chose him," Jasmin said. "He's charismatic enough to lead his men through Scylla and Charybdis without a mutiny. Not a lot of people could do that."

"I certainly couldn't," Alexandria agreed quickly.

The boat rocked as it hit its first patch of sand dunes. Everyone lurched forward, finding their footing again on the creaking wood. Hendrick ended the meeting, and the sailors returned to work, manning sails and rigging in order to anchor the boat. Instead of joining the men, Hendrick joined the heroes.

"How are you feeling about your task?" he asked. "I don't know what it is, but I will help you in whatever way I can, of course."

"We'll be fine," Josephine answered.

"Only wish Wen-Tang was with us," Brites added. "She would have been helpful..." She bit her lip so she didn't have to continue, and a heaviness settled over the group.

"I'm not a hero," Hendrick replied. "But now that she's gone–" he paused, trying to collect himself. "I am the senior ranking follower of Poseidon here... Ryn, in Olympia, sure, but I assume field command here. You have my full service, you know, if you need an extra pair of hands." As he spoke, he gazed steadily at Josephine, his eyes almost unblinking.

Alexandria felt a surge in her chest unlike the ones that had plagued her throughout the trip. They were not vicious, rage-ful, or disquieting; this was the steady, resolute jealousy that Josephine had managed to capture Hendrick's attention. She tried her best to quell the feeling by focusing on the task at hand. Soon, they would be entangled in the forest of a magical island, looking for a godly plant. One that Wen-Tang had sacri-ficed herself to the gods for them to find. *No crushes. You don't have time!* It was only fair to assume that the herb would not come easily; that the cost would be great.

Alexandria had not served the gods long, but she had served them long enough to know that. And feelings of jealousy couldn't stand in her way of the greater good.

Circe's Island stretched out from the docks, blocking the view of the horizon and the sunset. It seemed to capture all of the light inside of its forest, which glowed pink and red as the leaves swallowed light shafts and spat them back out upon the dunes. Waters lapped at the sand softly. It was like an inlet, calm and undisturbed by rough waters. Most of the island was forest. There was little sand, just enough to set up a tent or two. The rest was rough seagrass and gnarled, twisted roots of tall trees that guarded the precious inhabitants within. If she peered closely, Alexandria could make out shapes flitting around in the woods: nymphs and birds and all manners of creatures that lived there under Circe's protection. She wondered how Circe felt about their arrival. She did not doubt that their mission was not as secret as they might have hoped.

Alexandria rested her hands on the railing, listening as the boat creaked back and forth and thinking of the end of her conversation with Hendrick. The heroes, much to her dismay, had politely declined his help and assured him they would be more than capable of handling it on their own. She sighed.

She knew she would never see Hendrick again, certainly not in any way that was conducive to getting to know him. Her role as a hero and the demands of Olympia kept her far too busy to visit Alaska on any regular basis. And she remembered with distaste the way he had looked fondly at Josephine.

What does any of it matter? He doesn't like me anyway. I'm better off forgetting about him. Besides, I'm a hero of Olympia. I need to focus on my own stuff. I don't have time for a relationship. He's cute. Not cute enough.

The thought was painful, heartrending even; Alexandria could feel not just the bubbling jealousy, but also the deep-rooted anger that had plagued her during the entire trip. It was wrong, all of it was wrong. Her breathing felt short and tight. She wondered if this was how Wen-Tang had felt as she was going mad, or if it was something else.

Could Penthesilea's sword really have sped things up that much? It doesn't seem possible. Ares' other heroes served much longer than I have and didn't go mad until the end of it. Why would I be any different?

Her musings were cut short when Triniya placed a hand on

her shoulder. Alexandria looked over at her and Triniya nodded towards the island. "We're going to have to be careful not to offend Circe when we get off tomorrow. And we should be well-rested; we're fools if we think it'll be as easy as picking some moly."

"I'm not tired," Alexandria huffed. Grainy dusk settled over the island. "It's not late, either."

"Mm," Triniya hummed. "Time works weirdly around magical islands like this."

"Sure." Alexandria shrugged, turning to face Triniya properly, her back against the railing. She was tired of peering into the growing darkness of the island. It felt foreboding and terrifying without sunlight illuminating all of its corners. "But I'm not tired. I don't see the point of trying to go to bed if I'm not tired."

"I'm not trying to tell you what to do," Triniya replied calmly. "Promise. But we've all had a long day and we'll have another long tomorrow. I'm just trying to look out for you, really. I know you feel bad about Wen-Tang..."

"She's not dead," Alexandria snapped. "And I'm not dwelling on that, either. It doesn't matter. She made her choices, just like we all make choices."

Triniya put her hands up as if she were surrendering. "Are you okay?" she asked.

"I'm fine," Alexandria huffed, turning away again. The view of Circe's Island suddenly seemed more pleasant and endurable than Triniya's bewildered and hurt expression.

None of them understand. Besides, they had no problem talking amongst themselves and leaving me out before. Why won't they leave me alone now when I actually want it?

"Ok," Triniya said softly. "Make sure to go to bed soon then, I guess. I'll see you in the morning when we disembark. Goodnight, Alexandria."

Alexandria didn't answer, her fingers clutching the railing so hard her knuckles turned white. She felt her knees buckle underneath her and only held herself up with her arms. *What are the gods going to do to us?*

INTERLUDE
UNDERWATER

Day 14

It had been cold. That was the last thing that Wen-Tang remembered feeling. The deep, numbing sense of cold that froze her bones and chilled her heart. But now, a strange warmth came over her limbs and she felt the gentleness of someone's hand tracing her cheek. Her eyes fluttered open and then closed again, too heavy with weariness. A soothing voice whispered something in her ear, but she couldn't understand what it said, as she drifted back off into the world of dreams and visions.

When she woke, she jumped off whatever bed she was on and scurried out of the room. There was no one to stop her. The ground rocked underneath her rhythmically, and it steadied her heartbeat as she let that feeling sink into her bones. This part was familiar. She emerged on the deck of a ship she didn't recognize. It bore the same figurehead as the *Twin Delphinus*, but the ship was not the same. It looked older, more worn from years spent traveling the seas. The wood creaked under her feet as she traversed to the other side of the deck, leaning over the railing. The waters didn't look familiar, either: they were rougher and the rocks peeking out on the horizon were sharp and grey.

"We're not in Olympia," a voice said behind her.

She turned. Poseidon stood there, his hands crossed. He was dressed in a simple t-shirt and jeans, and he looked far younger. His hair, dark and curly, seemed shorter; his beard more trimmed. His eyes, twinkling and laughing, seemed simultaneously serious: he eyed her with concern, though he tried his best to hide it; she could tell.

"We're straddling worlds right now, Wen-Tang. This ship and these waters, my crew has not seen since millennia before the destruction. This is the original ship, the *Delphinus*, which shipwrecked long before her successor the *Twin Delphinus* would bear you as her commander. We are in the Atlantic Ocean, in the mortal world. Once, my pirates used to spend all their time in these rough waters, just beyond the reach of mortal sailors. But we abandoned it long ago. Strange, isn't it? To be so close to things you recognize and can almost grasp, but so far at the same time?"

"Why am I here?"

"You're healing, Wen-Tang. You did your very best to drown back in Alaska. That storm was designed to take you off course and bring you back to Olympia. You're lucky you were in the ocean for most of it; my power protected you from the most dangerous of it. And falling into the water was another blessing in disguise. I was able to hide you away from the other gods and now will bring you back to Atlantis to rest and recover."

Wen-Tang's hands balled into fists. "Why? Don't the gods intend to banish me back to the mortal world with no memories? Why would you care whether I lived or died?"

"I have no intention of doing what the council wishes,"

Poseidon answered. "I do not see a reason to get rid of my hero so soon. You have served me well and faithfully, Wen-Tang, and you are now royalty of Atlantis. You simply need time, and your body will adjust to the powers I have given it."

"I'm going mad," Wen-Tang snarled. She knew he was hiding something, she could hear it in his cadence. *There's no fixing the madness, there's no delaying it. He's gone crazy himself. He thinks he can save me.* "And you knew it would happen to me, but you clearly didn't care enough to tell me that becoming the princess of Atlantis might kill me."

"It wouldn't kill you," Poseidon said dismissively. "I would never allow it to come to that. If the need arose, perhaps I would send you back to the mortal world for some time, that you might recoup, but I would always bring you back to serve me until the end of your days. You will adjust to your powers. I know you will."

He sounds delusional, she thought. *Absolutely mad. Being the princess of Atlantis is what made this worse; I don't think it's going to somehow make me better, too. I can't be saved, I can feel it in my bones. He's not looking at things as they are.* "I don't believe you. The council of the gods would never let you disobey them."

"Not always, perhaps," Poseidon sighed. "But I hold enough sway at the moment, and you are not dangerous; you seem to... well, to have your condition under control. There's no reason they couldn't be persuaded, I think."

You know it's not under control. You know I might snap and kill you all at any moment. Why are you being so reckless? You can't possibly care for me that much. I can't be saved! You know it! I see it in your eyes!

"I will not beg to remain in Olympia if they wish to be rid of me," Wen-Tang retorted. "I will not be a suppliant asking to keep descending further into madness. That sounds like a terrible way to die. I would rather lose my memories and return to the mortal world and maybe live a life of dignity."

"Would you leave so easily?" Poseidon asked. Wen-Tang shrugged.

"I don't hold my power as dearly as I hold my honour."

And because you're lying when you say I'll heal. I will just self-destruct.

CHAPTER 17

CIRCE'S ISLAND

Day 15

The sand was warm and fine. It creeped into the small crevices of Josephine's shoes and tickled her toes as she sank in its softness until it covered up to her ankles. Her feet began to chafe as she started walking into the forest, following after the other heroes. She bent down and undid the laces, following the example of the others, who knocked their shoes against fallen timbers to clean them out. It was several minutes before they had all retied their shoes and were ready to continue walking.

The forest stretched out before them, appearing not quite real. All the colors were slightly too brilliant, the greens slightly too vibrant. Yellow and red birds flitted between the branches, like jewels sparkling in the sun. Their merry tunes filled the soft breezes, carrying with them the sounds of the water hitting the sands and gulls crying out around the boat. The bright sun filtered down through palm leaves in mottled patterns. Small creatures scurried to and fro: squirrels, possums, rabbits, and small foxes that slinked away warily.

Josephine soon found herself in the middle of the pack, lodged between Brites, who appeared to be purposefully ignoring her, and Triniya, who smiled every time she caught her eye. For all the strides that Josephine had made with her peers, there was still the distinct coldness of memories: that she did not really belong with them, that they were enemies who were collaborating out of necessity, that once they had found the moly plant and returned to Alaska, Josephine would probably be brought to Olympia and put on trial for plotting against the gods.

The chill in the air raised goosebumps on her skin. While on the boat, Josephine had almost been able to forget about the strange, convoluted stance she held compared to the other heroes. Hendrick had treated her deferentially and kindly and made no distinctions between her side and his side.

It was a nice break, she thought, as Triniya began sharing some joke with her, trying to ignore Brites' frowns. *If I had more time, maybe I could have fallen in love with him.* He was kind and gentle, and an attractive young man. But Josephine knew his gentility towards her hadn't gone unnoticed. She had caught Alexandria's eye as they descended from the ship and could feel the anger burning in her gaze. Alexandria liked Hendrick; Josephine was sure of that. When Hendrick called the meeting and they were all gathered in front of him, Josephine had noticed how Alexandria could hardly take her eyes off of him.

It's too bad she'll never have him. It's worse that I never will. The idea of vying with Alexandria for a boy almost sounded thrilling to Josephine. *Like we're just teenagers in our own little worlds. Not heroes grappling against each other for the gods.*

James' face flashed before her eyes, as he had appeared on the beach before the whole mess had begun. The way his hair was swept to the side by the breeze from the water, his stormy gray eyes, the feel of his hand on the small of her back as he ensured she didn't trip over rocks. How could she have forgotten him so easily? *It's only been a couple weeks.* James had done everything for her, laid himself at her feet. When she was new to the demands of tactics and strategizing, he had been her guide and help as she navigated her new role.

Having recalled him, she felt a heavy weight in her chest as she realized how much she missed him. How much she missed her life as Athena's hero. Her role there was clear and defined and she was immersed in the intellectual milieu that she craved.

And now look at me. I'm tromping through the woods with a bunch of horrible idiots looking for an herb to keep us from gong mad.

A crash in front of her brought her back to reality. A tree had just fallen in front of her, Triniya, and Brites. Alexandria and Jasmin were on the other side of it, only visible by the tops of their heads.

"Are you okay?" Jasmin shouted. Fingertips appeared, hovering over the top of the trunk but disappeared just as quickly. It was too large to climb over.

"We're fine!" Brites answered. Josephine frowned at the strain she heard in the other girl's voice. *Maybe she's not simply mad at me.*

"Good! Do you think you could crawl under the tree?"

"Not really," Triniya said as she got on her hands and knees and looked through the brush. "There isn't a big enough gap."

"Keep going," Brites said. "The moly grows around Circe's house. We'll walk around the tree and meet you there but there's no point in delaying our mission for this."

"Are you sure?" Jasmin. "Is breaking up really a smart idea?"

"It'll be fine! What's the worst that could happen?" Brites answered. "I've been here before; I'm sure I can find my way to Circe's again."

There was silence from the other side and then the sound

of tramping through the woods started up again and became quieter and quieter, fading away. Josephine eyed the two other girls. She could feel the tension in the air, but she couldn't tell if it was directed at her or not.

"What's the plan?" Josephine asked, shattering the silence. She saw Brites sigh in relief that she'd spoken.

"To go around, I guess," Triniya replied. "Hopefully the tree wasn't as large as it sounded." She led the way, walking down the length of the tree towards the roots. After only a handful of minutes, they reached the end of the massive palm and then turned to continue straight and catch up with Alexandria and Jasmin. Brites took over the lead from Triniya, weaving through pockets of trees and empty glades, completely overrun by various birds and wildlife and hundreds of species of flowers, always working her way towards the magical lights of Circe's palace in the distance. Somehow, they sparkled and shone, even in the bright sun. Triniya matched her pace with Josephine and kept tilting her head to look at the other girl. Eventually, Josephine held her gaze. *I'm not going to talk first,* she told herself.

"What are you going to do when we get back?"

The question caught Josephine off-guard. She peered at the Vestal Virgin searchingly. Perhaps she should have known it was coming. It hung over all of them: whether Josephine would return to Athena and rejoin her forces, whether she'd stick it out with the heroes, or whether she'd go back to the mortal world and try to return to a normal life. Of course, she'd have to convince them not to put her on trial in front of the other gods for any of those decisions to work.

"Well... this is assuming you're not going to tie me up and drag me to Olympia for a trial. But I haven't decided yet," she said warily. "I don't think Athena's simply going to accept my return and forgive me for having betrayed her in London. I might be better off trying to make it on my own."

A shadow passed over Triniya's face. "You shouldn't do that," she stated forcefully. "It never ends well for a hero who has no allegiance to a god. You should come back to Olympia and make your home there, with us."

"Are you referring to Keilee?" Josephine raised an eyebrow. Triniya blushed. "They speak of it among the Warriors. I've heard the story from James."

"James?"

"My..." Josephine swallowed. She wasn't sure what James was anymore. He'd been her boyfriend since she became Athena's hero, but now she'd betrayed him and his people. Would he still want her? Would he still trust her? Even if he did, could she go back? "It's unimportant." Hendrick's face flashed before her eyes. "He's another one of the Warriors; he serves on the council. He was responsible for initiating me into the world of the gods."

"Ah," Triniya said knowingly, as if she could sense everything churning inside of Josephine's head. Her smile seemed gentle, almost like she wanted Josephine to feel comfortable with her. "I see."

Josephine answered, "This mission is just as important. It won't do your Virgins any good if you're going mad. It certainly won't do Alexandria any good if we don't get the moly. Wen-Tang too, if she's still alive."

"Alexandria?"

"Haven't you noticed?" Josephine said. Brites stopped and turned around to face Josephine. The three girls loosely formed a circle, looking at each other warily.

"Noticed what?" Brites demanded.

"Alexandria is teetering on the verge of madness. She's not there yet, like Wen-Tang, but I can see it when I look at her—not that I told her; I told her I didn't think she was having that issue. Figured that was safer. You haven't noticed?" Josephine's eyebrows furrowed. "I would have thought you knew. You've certainly known her longer than I have."

Silence followed her comment. She shook her head.

"She moves stiffly when she's angry, like she's trying to keep herself from doing something rash. Her eyes go dark and her temper is more volatile. All signs– I saw it on the boat, with Hendrick. He spoke to me during the assembly and I could feel her gaze." Josephine inadvertently shivered. "She looked as if she wanted to kill me and could only barely restrain herself from it."

"I find that hard to believe." Brites shook her head, her eyes clouding over slightly. "I would have noticed if something was happening to Alexandria."

"None of you knew when Wen-Tang was affected. You see what you want to see, Brites. It's your flaw," Josephine scowled. "The same way you can't help seeing me as an enemy that might betray you at any moment even though I've done all in my power to help with this mission."

Brites drew her knife and pounced on Josephine, holding it to her throat. "Don't talk to me like that. No matter how much you help us, you're still one of Athena's Warriors. You're actively trying to destroy Olympia. My best friend just died trying to preserve it. How *dare* you speak to me of flaws."

Josephine pressed the tip of her own blade against Brites' stomach. They stood there, locked in a silent battle of wills, neither one willing to be the first to surrender or to fight. Triniya watched them with wide eyes, unsure of what to do.

"Brites, back off," she whispered, but the other girl ignored her. Josephine locked eyes with Triniya. In that moment, they came to the same conclusion. *Brites isn't doing well, either.*

It dragged on for what seemed like an interminable amount of time. The cold of Brites' blade warmed until Josephine could barely tell it apart from her own skin. Her dagger remained pressed against Brites' stomach, but her fingers began to cramp from the strong grip she held it with.

"Are you two done?" Triniya finally asked, trying to sound lighthearted. "I hate to break it up, but we've actually got to find the moly plant."

As if obeying a command, the two girls pulled apart and sheathed their weapons. *I need to watch out while I'm around Brites,* Josephine decided. *She's the only one of these heroes who wouldn't hesitate to run me through with a sword if she got the chance.*

"We've got to catch up with the other two," Triniya said, taking over the lead from Brites in a flurry of activity. "Thanks to your little spat, we've fallen even more behind."

CHAPTER 18
CIRCE'S HOUSE

Day 15

Alexandria snuck around the edge of the garden, peering in, looking for what she might recognize as the moly plant from the book Josephine had shown them. Jasmin was behind her, also looking intently. They could not find it in one of the carefully cultivated beds of flowers and herbs, nor was it immediately discernible amongst the overgrowth of weeds and greenery along the back of the garden. It teemed with birds, butterflies, and bees, who all scattered when Alexandria hopped the fence and began carefully looking through the wild plants.

Bright colors glimmered in the sunlight: the reds, oranges, pinks, and purples of flowers, the tall, sneaking vines of ivy and honeysuckle. Alexandria's head spun with the hundreds of blooms and plants growing around her. The air was sickly sweet from their scents, a mix of roses, gardenias, and holly. Large palm trees covered the old stone house, with its various turrets and faded pink shingles. The house, Alexandria thought, looked like a cross between a castle and a haunted house. *Not what I would've thought Circe would live in. Maybe she updates it every couple of centuries or something.*

"Careful," Jasmin said. "We don't want Circe to think we're up to no good. She might turn us into pigs."

Alexandria scoffed. "She's not going to turn us into pigs, Jasmin."

"You might think that, but in the Odyssey... well, that's a book. I guess it's possible those events were made up for the sake of telling a better story. But Hendrick and his crew have had a bad run-in with Circe, too. Remember when the crew told us of that one time–"

"I doubt it would happen to us," Alexandria interrupted. She didn't want to be reminded about the crew turning into pigs. She was trying to avoid that mental picture. Her hands brushed the leaves of a small, round plant with prickly edges. *Moly.* It was short and unobtrusive; no wonder she hadn't been able to see it from outside the garden. It was hidden in the tall grasses and flowers. She began plucking sprigs of it and stuffing them into her pockets.

"What do we have here?" a voice thundered behind her. Alexandria whirled around. Towering over her was a beautiful young woman, with golden hair braided into a crown around her face, tussled and worn from a day of wandering the woods. A small crown of flowers rested on top of the braid. Her cheeks were flushed and pink; her black eyes dark and terrible; her soft, pale skin only hinted at a sunburn. Her arms were crossed over her chest as she observed the thief calmly. Alexandria hadn't even heard her approach.

"Circe," she breathed.

Jasmin came tramping through the garden to her rescue. "My lady," she said, bowing. "We mean you no harm, nor do we come with bad intentions. We merely seek some of the moly you cultivate in your garden."

"Why," Circe asked, "would heroes of the gods want moly plant unless it was to harm me and my nymphs? I have not forgotten how Odysseus also came in peace, with the blessings of Athena and Hermes. I have no love for the gods or their heroes. Your status will not protect you here."

"We'll leave," Alexandria offered. "We'll head back to the ship right now."

Circe laughed. It was a horrible, dry laugh that rattled Alexandria's bones and fried her nerves. "What kind of a goddess would I be if I simply let you go from my grasp? Let you escape back to Olympia unpunished for your trespassing and stealing?" She looked pointedly at Alexandria's pockets, filled with moly. "I have maintained my domain only through the use of force. My nymphs are safe because I do not shy away from using my magic to keep them so. Letting you go would encourage others to come hunting for whatever they wanted on my island, and my people and I would be slaughtered. I cannot countenance that."

"Circe..." Jasmin started. She was interrupted as Circe pointed her finger at her and a cloud of smoke appeared. When it settled, Alexandria stared into the eyes of a pig, frantically screaming, "Oink! Oink!"

Horror closed her throat and she couldn't scream, even as she tried. *Oh my gods, I'm going to be a pig!*

Even though panic filled her, she refused to let Circe see it. Giving away her weakness to her opponent wouldn't get them out of this mess. "You won't touch me, Circe," she said with more confidence than she felt. "I am the hero of Ares, I am the Queen of the Amazons– and I will not be turned into a pig!"

"I cannot touch you, Alexandria, hero of Ares, for you bear the moly plant that shields from all enchantments. You are free to go, but your companion has to stay. Will you leave her to roam my garden and roll around in dirt for all eternity? Can you put your mission and the safety of all of the other heroes before your friend beside you?"

Alexandria reached for the moly in her pocket.

"I know why you've come to steal it," Circe continued. "You hope to stave off the madness of the gods with it and to defend yourself against their powers. I knew long before you arrived on this island. They sent me a message, asking me to aid them by capturing the heroes and returning them to Olympia. In exchange, I will be given a seat on the council and finally honoured as the goddess that I am. I couldn't possibly pass up a deal like that, could I? I'm willing to dismiss the past trespasses of the gods for a position of authority."

Jasmin's oinks grew more distressed. She seemed to be trying to tell Alexandria what to do, but Alexandria couldn't figure out whether it was that she should run, leave the pig behind, and warn the others, or if Jasmin was begging her to save her, somehow.

Regardless, Alexandria knew she couldn't leave Jasmin behind. She would never be able to live with herself if she did. It would haunt her forever. And the other heroes would never forgive her, either. Jasmin was one of them far more than Alexandria was and had been a constant source of affection and encouragement since she'd taken up the mantle of Oracle.

"You won't leave her," Circe said. "We both know you won't. And you won't hurt me, either, as much as you might wish to. You can't let the other heroes know you're losing your mind just like Wen-Tang. It scares you, doesn't it, my dear? That you've already lost your mind... hand over the moly, and I'll turn you into a pig so you can join your friend. The enchantment won't last long, don't worry. The gods will undo it before they put you on trial for treason to Olympia. It will slow down the madness, too... wouldn't that be nice?"

A drumming sound filled her head as her eyes glazed over

and her focus faded. In one swift move, she unsheathed her sword. *Don't call me mad!* The moly would protect her, which meant she had the upper hand. *I'm not mad- I'm not mad, you can't bait me with that.*

I won't let you get away with calling me that.

"I won't run," she growled. "And I won't give you the moly. This is your last warning to let us go."

Her face contorted into an angry, red blob. Alexandria held out her sword, brandishing it front of her like a shield.

Circe snarled, all calm pretenses vanishing from her face. "That stupid plant! Hand it over!" She lunged for the girl, but Alexandria scrambled away, with her sword still protecting her. She made a move to slash at Circe, but the goddess stepped to the side before she had the chance. Another flick of her finger, as if it were an automatic reflex. Alexandria felt nothing. She went on the offensive, methodically slashing away, forcing Circe to dance her way back as the point of the sword moved forward. No blood was drawn, but Alexandria slowly began to win ground. It felt like no time at all before she finally had Circe cornered against the wall of her own house.

Alexandria smiled. Jasmin the pig was at her feet, oinking incessantly at Circe. "Turn her back into a human," Alexandria demanded.

"You can't make me."

The sword pressed against Circe's throat. "Try me." Alexandria felt her world go fuzzy as her focus seemed to sharpen on every angle of Circe's face. Nothing else mattered. Jasmin's oinks faded, too, leaving Alexandria in a silent world. The only sound was the faint heartbeat of Circe pounding in fear.

"You're scared," Alexandria said. Even to her, her voice sounded dark and strange, unlike her own. Every minute detail and change in Circe's face was magnified. "You may be immortal, but you are not invincible. What have the gods said they would do to you if you failed to bring us to them?"

"That's none of your business." Circe's voice shook. "You've gone mad, Alexandria, you aren't seeing reason. You can't kill me. Your sword can't harm me. If I took away the moly from you, I could turn you into any animal I wished."

"Try, then." Alexandria pressed the blade enough to puncture Circe's skin. Droplets of blood stained the top of her white peplos. "You wouldn't dare."

"Listen to me," Circe said, her tone shifting. "Let's discuss this, Alexandria. I'm not your enemy. I have my gripes with the Olympians just as much as you do– they have not been my friends over the years. I wish you no harm, truly. I'm trying to help you. I have watched heroes go mad before. They are happier once they have been set free from the bonds of magic and oaths."

"I don't believe you," Alexandria snarled. "You want the moly. You want your seat on Olympus. Don't *lie* to me."

"Listen to me, please," Circe begged. "This isn't you speaking. It's the madness... it has taken over your mind! You have to believe me. I have seen what happens to heroes... and the same will happen to you, Alexandria. Though your time has been brief. Clearly, you're simply a weaker mortal who couldn't handle the magic as well as others might. Ares will simply pick herself a new hero."

"No." Alexandria's voice reverberated across the garden, just as the other heroes came bounding through. They stopped when they saw Alexandria and stumbled back. Alexandria tried to imagine herself as she looked down at the other heroes. In her head, she was taller, and menacing. It was as if she had grown several inches in her terror. A dark cloud seemed to cling to her edges, as it if was starting to consume her.

"I told you she was going mad," Josephine said.

Alexandria snarled at her. *I'm not mad. How does no one see? There is no other way. Circe will not help us. I'm merely protecting everyone. She needs to turn Jasmin back into a human and then I will let her go.*

"Stop her," Circe begged the other heroes. "She won't listen to me. I'll give you safe passage off my island if you take her away. She needs to be brought before the council. It's not safe for Olympia for them to be part of its forces."

Alexandria, in a fit of rage, thrust her sword into Circe's stomach. The goddess gasped. Her face drained of colour. Everyone around her screamed. Josephine lunged at her and wrestled the weapon away, pulling it out of Circe, who sunk to the ground. Alexandria didn't fight her. She suddenly felt entirely devoid of energy, like everything was collapsing in on her. Breathing was hard. She fell to her knees, struggling to catch her breath.

Brites caught her arm and yanked her back onto her feet. "We have to go, now," she whispered. "This is not the time for you to feel faint."

"I've got the moly," Triniya said, coming to join the rest of them. In her hand, she clutched the preciously-won herbs. Alexandria thought of the other small bunches in her pocket but couldn't muster the strength to say anything.

"Let's get out of here before we make matters any worse," Josephine declared. She scooped up Jasmin the pig and they set from the garden, taking the most direct route they could manage back to the ship. No one spoke.

INTERLUDE
ONBOARD

They sat in the captain's quarters, forming a loose circle. Triniya still held the moly in her hand, but no one paid attention to it. Everyone was focused on Alexandria. She leaned against Brites, still catching her breath, her face pale and lined with exhaustion. They did not press her with questions or chatter around her. The entire cabin was hushed.

"I don't know what happened," Alexandria said, laboriously and quietly. "I didn't think I would stab her."

"She'll live," Brites assured her. "She's immortal. You did nothing more than cause her a slight inconvenience. But Jasmin's still a pig. We haven't solved that yet."

"And we have the moly," Triniya added. "The mission was a success."

"It's too late for me," Alexandria said despondently. "I've already gone mad. I should take a boat out to sea, just like Wen-Tang did."

The ship rocked back and forth, shifting the streaming lights in the cabin. First, they bore down upon the coffee table, with its handful of books scattered around. Next, they illuminated the shelves, with their cabinet doors locked tight to prevent anything from spilling out. There were heaps of rolled maps, brass compasses, and wooden spyglasses with gold filigree all piled in haphazardly, as if they had been collected over the years but never cared for. Then, the sun reflected against the curtains, getting caught in the patterns of the silver embroidery against the dark blue. The boat was still anchored at the island, but the hum of preparations to leave could be heard on the deck.

"You'll be fine," Triniya said. "The gods won't be able to get rid of you now that we have the moly. And I'm sure that the madness is reversible somehow..."

"Or at least, more realistically, it'll just fade over time if you're less exposed to the gods. Now that the sword of Penthesilea is no longer controlling you," Brites pointed out, "you're being inundated with less power. Over time, I'm sure the effects will start to wear off."

An awed whisper, "The sword of Penthesilea? You've seen it?" came from Josephine. "I've only read about it... what does it look like in real life?"

"We don't talk about it," Alexandria snapped. "It's better off destroyed, if you ask me."

Josephine's face fell. "Why?"

"It was a danger to Olympia," Triniya answered far more kindly. "And it was being used to control Ares' heroes. If Penthesilea had known it was controlling her, she would have ordered it to be destroyed."

"Can we finish this conversation later?" Alexandria interrupted. "We've got bigger problems than that. Jasmin is *still* a pig and I stabbed Circe in the stomach. She might be trapped on her island, but she'll find a way to pay us back for that. And the gods are still after us– so if we could figure out any of those while we wait to set sail, that would be fantastic."

"Alexandria is correct," Brites grumbled. "The first thing to do is for all of us to take some of the moly and carry it. Triniya, if you would."

Triniya handed out sprigs of moly to the other heroes, one by one.

"We don't have time to go looking for Wen-Tang. We'll have to assume she's dead," Josephine said. "I know it's hard, but either she'll make it on her own or the gods will bring her to trial. We won't be able to rescue her."

"Don't say it," Triniya whispered, her voice tremulous.

"If we didn't have to deal with your goddess' betrayal," Brites snapped, "then we could head straight to Olympia and save Wen-Tang."

"Oink, oink!" said Jasmin.

"And Jasmin is still a pig!" Alexandria pointed out.

"One problem at a time," Josephine countered.

"Don't tell us what to do," Brites argued.

"Oink!"

"Arguing isn't going to do us any good," Triniya replied.

"Not arguing, just stating a fact," Alexandria said.

"We all know Jasmin's a pig, but none of us have an idea what to do about it," Brites snapped.

"I was just saying, maybe we should focus on trying to find a solution for that," Alexandria shot back.

"She's not wrong," Triniya said. "Jasmin's been leading this entire mission. I don't know if we can do this without her."

"You're the one who just told us not to argue and now you're taking sides," Brites huffed. "I think we should start with stopping Athena first."

"Oink!"

"While dragging a pig along with us?" Josephine stood up, gesturing towards Jasmin. "That's insane."

Brites also stood up. "You're not going to help us stop Athena, so I don't see why you're even still on this boat."

"Guys, this isn't a productive–" Alexandria stood up, ready

to keep the two of them from going at each other. A sudden rap on the door prevented the scene from escalating any further. She sighed with relief when Hendrick poked his head in.

"We're about to cast off," he said, his eyes roaming over the girls. Alexandria became acutely aware of how strange they looked. A small pig on the couch, huddled underneath the lanky arm of Triniya; Brites and Josephine, red in the face, prepared to square each other off, and Alexandria with her arms out to stop them. She blushed. It was not the impression she wanted to make on Hendrick, whose blue eyes seemed to pierce her.

Blood rushed to her head and ears when his gaze finally alighted on Josephine, not her.

"I don't know what you all did," he said slowly. "But a nymph from Circe has just arrived and told us we are no longer welcome on the island." He glanced at Jasmin quizzically. "I hope you got whatever it is you were hoping for."

CHAPTER 19
ATLANTIS

Day 16

The waters glimmered in the soft light that descended to the depths of the ocean. Atlantis stood like a crown upon a brow, tall and strong, nestled amongst coral reefs that teemed with life. Fish fluttered back and forth, darting in and out of various shadowy hiding spots. A pair of Spanish dancers swam up to Wen-Tang and peered at her curiously through their bug-like eyes. She inclined her head to them, and they bowed back, fluttering away idly back into the crowds of creatures. Atlantis always hummed with the activity of its surroundings: here were the freshest waters, the best food, the safest reefs to raise families in. Wen-Tang's eyes kept darting from species to species as she tried to catalogue them all in her mind. She did not swim into them; Poseidon's hand tightly gripped her own.

"You will not leave the perimeters of my domain," he said once they arrived at the gates of Olympus. Far above them, the opalescent pearl-studded walls rose, with their intricate gates composed of intertwined corals. "I am taking a risk even having you in my kingdom at the moment, Wen-Tang. The other gods will consider it an act of war."

"Then-"

"Silence, Captain. As I was saying, the gods will consider it an act of war, but it is a maneouver I am willing to make. I have already told you how I will defend you in front of the council when the need arises, and that I will not release you from my service. To argue is pointless. However, I do not wish to antagonize the other gods until it cannot be avoided. And so you will stay out of sight, quiet, until I tell you otherwise."

"I'm basically a prisoner," Wen-Tang grumbled.

"Do not be silly," Poseidon frowned. "It is not an imprisonment. I am trying to keep you safe. Your bounds are the bounds of Atlantis. Do not worry, I will keep you busy. You still have not completed your training as the Princess of Atlantis. There is much for you to learn about the ways of my kingdom. You will meet with my diplomats, observe my council meetings, and read the laws and regulations of our society. You'll have hours of uninterrupted time to do so, I'm sure."

Wen-Tang's scowl deepened. At this particular moment, there was nothing she wished to do less than listen to old council members drone for hours about a nitpicky economic incentive. The madness boiling in her veins drove her– to do something, to hurt something, to feel the rage and the power of blood shedding. The thought crossed her mind as she looked at a pack of dolphins pass by the edges of the gates, which slowly began to open before her. They creaked under the weight of their decorations and the water currents swooshed by, pushing Wen-Tang and Poseidon into the city. The gates slammed shut behind them with a final groan.

"Welcome back to Atlantis, Princess Wen-Tang."

"I don't want to hear it." Wen-Tang finally managed to wrench her wrist away. She floated down a side street, leaving

Poseidon behind. It was unfamiliar to her, like most of the streets in Atlantis. Last time she'd been here, she'd spent most of her time meandering through the castle halls, peeking into old libraries and nosing around the kitchens and gardens.

It was an adorable little street, with its tiny houses of various shapes lining the shell-covered sidewalk. Fish and dolphins swam around her as she tried to navigate out of the traffic, onto the sidewalk meant for the merpeople swimming to the shops. The houses– blue contraptions with white or red roofs– turned into a commercial square, buzzing with shoppers, all chatting in high voices. Shops crowded the street, and merpeople weaved in and out of them, arms loaded with large shopping bags. Two women passed by her, eagerly discussing the latest jewelry they'd selected for a party that night.

I don't know what he's up to, but it's not good. He's lying to himself, I know it– I can't be fixed. It's not possible. I can see it, I can feel it– is he just trying to destroy me by having me stay here? Does he really think I can be saved? Why would he think that if it's never happened before in the history of Olympia?

She swam back down the road, to where she'd run away from Poseidon. He was no longer standing there, but in front of her were the courtyards and front gardens of the Palace of Atlantis. She gazed up at it, recalling the feeling of seeing it for the first time. It had been far more overwhelming, seemed far more imposing. Wen-Tang watched it diminish in her eyes, coming down to just another paltry castle for another paltry god. She was thankful Poseidon had decided to protect her from the other gods, but she was wary, regardless.

I can't figure out why he's doing it. It can't just be because he likes me as his hero. The blood boiling in her body urged her to attack him, forcing him to reveal his motivations, even though she knew logically it would do nothing.

"I'll figure it out," she told herself, swimming into the courtyard and to the side entrance of the palace. It seemed to Wen-

Tang that Poseidon preferred to live as un-ostentatiously as he could manage. Everyone entered through side doors and hidden work entrances. Meals were delivered to rooms and never held in state at the banquet hall. Most of the time, Wen-Tang forgot she wasn't alone in the palace. Everything seemed to happen by magic, quietly, invisibly.

She pulled the door closed behind her. The smells of the kitchen wafted through the hallway enticing her towards the right and its various doors, all hiding culinary delights. The smell of roasted meats and vegetables, and the sweetness of pies and cakes, were far more arousing than anything she'd ever smelled. Wen-Tang eagerly followed her nose, until she shortly found herself standing at the edge of a kitchen with a small pie in her hands, chatting to the cook who'd made it about the comings and goings of Atlantis.

Lord Zeus had recently visited. Wen-Tang's eyebrows raised. It had been only days after his return to Olympia, if the cook's math was correct, so it couldn't have had anything to do with the madness infecting her. *But,* Wen-Tang thought back to Akira and Aphrodite's return and all the news she'd heard about the North Guard, *it probably has something to do with the war against Atar. I wonder if it was an alliance thing or if Zeus was just making sure the gods would support him.* For the rest of the conversation, she let the cook's words wash over her and didn't listen; she thought about Atar and the North Guard and how Ryn must be leading the Pirates in battle. Kora briefly crossed her mind.

I wonder how she's handling having to face her brother, Wen-Tang thought. *I hope Ryn is keeping an eye on her.*

Briefly, she considered hunting Poseidon down and asking for permission to lead her Pirates, resuming control as the Captain. She dispelled the idea as soon as it came to her: no one knew she had returned to Olympia and furthermore, the gods were after her. It would be a disservice to the Pirates if she appeared. Instead, she settled on asking Poseidon for an update on the situation whenever she saw him next. She wanted to be dismissed from service due to the madness growing within her, but she also wished to know the people she cared about would be okay when she left.

CHAPTER 20
ALASKA (AGAIN)

Day 15

They found themselves at the same table in the same inn. It hadn't changed a lot, though wearily, Josephine felt as if everything had changed. The trip to Circe's Island had been, by all accounts, a disaster. Wen-Tang was gone. Jasmin was a pig. Alexandria was mad. Circe would be trying to kill them all if she ever got the chance. The only silver lining to the whole affair was that the moly had been secured.

Josephine's hand squeezed around her sprig of it, tucked away in her pocket. She needed to figure out a way to evade the heroes and escape back to Athena. She eyed them all, as they sat there silently. Half of them shivered from the cold and the other half gingerly sipped on hot soups. Jasmin was hidden under the table, smuggled in so the owner didn't turn her away.

A strange feeling of companionship washed over her. For all her enmity with these people, she'd faced several challenges with them, and they had not sacrificed her to protect themselves. Even Brites, who looked as if she might try and stab her at any moment, held a begrudging respect for her. Josephine could see it in the Huntress's eyes.

For a long time, no one spoke. The journey back had not been harrowing. *In fact*, Josephine thought to herself, *it was relatively calm.* No great storms had belied the anger of the gods, no nymphs had chased them across the waters to avenge Circe. Hendrick had easily sailed them through Scylla and Charybdis. He wished her goodbye when they disembarked. Josephine could still feel the indent his warm hand made on her hollow, cold skin. The starry gaze of his eyes was burned into her memory, and she could feel a blush creeping into her cheeks. In another life, perhaps she could have loved him for more than a handful of days; perhaps she even could have stayed on that ship with him for many years. But it was not to be. She knew that.

Her allegiance to Athena set her apart from all of the other heroes and followers in Olympia. Because of her goddess' machinations, Josephine was forbidden from mixing with her peers: she was marooned on the island of the Warriors. *It kind of sucks,* she thought. Until she'd been adventuring through trials with other heroes, she hadn't realized what she'd been missing. The intellect and books she'd been gifted as Athena's hero was starting to pale in comparison to what she could have if things were different. *James is nice but it's not the same as having a whole crew watching your back.*

The silence continued to pervade the atmosphere. Josephine could feel the weight of Brites' gaze hanging over her, as the Huntress slowly sipped her soup and nibbled on her bread. She was waiting for something, but Josephine wasn't sure what. Nor could she be bothered to ponder it, too busy considering her own weighty matters.

What do I do? She thought to herself. When faced with it, the idea of betraying the girls sitting around the table with her felt impossible. They had treated her with the respect due to a hero, even if they did not love or accept her. She was their equal in a way she was to no other followers. Her entire body felt as if it were in turmoil, ripping and tearing at itself from the inside.

The inn melted away from her gaze, shifting into a concoction of her mind. It retained the same wooden beams and heavy rafters, but they warped and bent in strange ways, like vines crawling up trellises. The heat from the fire fluttered around the room in colourful ways that shattered glass cabinets and cups. The faces of the people surrounding her were no longer recognizable. Brites' face melted away; Triniya's broke in half. Alexandria's faded into the darkness. All their eyes turned yellow and grew to the size of dinner plates. Their black pupils narrowed into the slits of owls. Beaks appeared in shadowy forms until suddenly Josephine was surrounded by owls and not humans.

They hooted at her, flapping their wings and causing a ruckus as they circled around her, tightening their formation. She was trapped in the middle of them and quickly became overwhelmed: they swallowed her up and trampled her under their scaly claws until she could see no more.

"Josephine! Josephine!" Triniya shook her shoulder, and Josephine groaned as her eyes fluttered open. "Are you alright? You scared the crap out of us, going along and fainting like that! What happened?" Josephine blinked wearily at the other girls crowding over her.

"Don't bombard her with questions." Brites rolled her eyes. "She needs a minute to come to."

"I'm alright, I'm alright..." Josephine struggled back onto her feet. During her strange altercation with the owls, she'd fallen back off her chair, onto the ground. Brites helped her sit down again and she sank back in the chair, feeling overwhelmed with exhaustion. "I don't know what happened; I might just have been faint."

"You should eat something." Triniya pushed a bowl of soup in front of her. "You haven't touched any food since we got back."

Brites raised an eyebrow at Josephine, as if she were trying to read her inner thoughts. Josephine shuddered. She couldn't help herself from seeing the owl face superimposed on Brites.

"What did you see?" Brites asked. She crossed her arms, as if she were trying to stare her down. "You kept groaning like you were in pain."

Josephine blushed. "I don't know what you're talking about. I didn't see anything."

"I can tell when you're lying," Brites answered. "Look. You might as well tell us. Like it or not, you've become embroiled with us and our shenanigans. You've thrown your lot with us, for better or for worse. You can save us a hell of a lot of trouble if you'd stop being so obstinate and start working with us as a teammate. What's Athena going to do to you when you go running back to her, anyway? Welcome you with open arms?"

"I don't know what you're talking about..."

"If you would just stop being so stubborn," Brites snapped. She threw her arms in the air and sank back into a chair. "I don't know what to do with you, Josephine. I've tried everything. We can't let you go back to Athena, not with how much you know about us. It would put all of us at risk. If you won't cooperate, I'll have to kill you. Damn the trial with the gods."

Josephine heard a sharp gasp. Her mind, already swimming with everything she'd just seen, tried to understand what Brites was threatening. *Everything gone. Just like that, like it all meant nothing. Her entire life, over.*

She wondered if she was strong enough to face death. Could she be loyal enough to her goddess to hold the information close to her chest, to stay secretive to the bitter end? Her palms grew sweaty as she tightened her hands into fists. Her forehead was drenched. Her hair stuck to her cheeks. *I can't do it. I'm a coward. I don't want to die. I don't want to die.*

"I don't want to die," she whispered.

Brites did not let anyone else speak. She glared at Triniya, who seemed ready to jump up and hold Josephine in her arms. Alexandria stood up, arms crossed, her eyes dark, but Josephine couldn't tell if her stormy face was directed at her or at Brites.

"It is entirely up to you what happens," Brites said. "Cooperate with us, give us the information we desire, and we will let you live. You will come with us to Olympia, and I will guarantee your safety and a spot on the council of heroes. Refuse to cooperate, however... you'd be a fool to cling so tightly to Athena, Josephine. What has she done for you?"

"Nothing," Josephine mumbled. It was true. *Athena hasn't tried to rescue me. She hasn't sent me a single message or sent any Warriors after me. It's like she's forgotten that I exist. Like she's replaced me already with another hero and accepted that I am dead to her. She won't take me back, she won't. Not after all I've done to help the heroes. I've betrayed her. I've thrown my lot in with the heroes. I have no other option. I have nowhere else to turn to.*

"I'll tell you," she finally said. It was as if an invisible cloud hung over them, insulating them from the rest of the inn, which had continued on its merry old business. Soups and drinks were served, and people cheered and told stories, seemingly oblivious to the storm brewing between the heroes.

Brites' face lightened. "Then let's get started. We have no time to waste. Tell us everything you know about Athena's plans to invade Olympia."

Swallowing hard, Josephine tried to clear her thoughts and her throat. She picked up her spoon with a trembling hand and sipped on her now lukewarm stew. "Where do you want me to start?"

"Wherever you think is best," Brites said, as they all settled around the table again, calmly taking their seats.

"The plan at first was to invade as soon as we had enough Warriors to muster a force. Athena was hoping to establish herself as the new ruler of Olympia before Zeus returned and reclaimed the throne for himself– really, she was hoping to beat Ares to finding a hero. But then," Josephine nodded towards Alexandria, "you came along. And we didn't have enough followers anyway, so we bided our time. Zeus returned much sooner than we expected, and we weren't sure what to do about it. So, we waited, to see how his arrival might upturn things in Olympia.

"None of us expected a war to break out between Olympia and the North Guard. That was a complete surprise, and obviously, it put all of our previous plans to rest. Everything was in shambles at that point, and we quickly had to figure out a new plan. It was decided that the smartest thing to do would be to let the North Guard and Olympia destroy each other. If there were less followers to contend with when we invaded, it would only make things easier for us. And of course, the North Guard would play into our hand either way. If they won, then Athena could style herself as the liberator of Olympia and justify her invasion that way. If they lost, well, then, we wouldn't have to worry about them in the future.

"Athena knew that the other gods would send people to stop her. But your arrivals were a surprise to us. We thought the heroes would stay and manage Olympia and send their seconds to the mortal world. It wasn't clear whether we could defeat you on our own, so Athena forged an alliance with Hades. Hades was supposed to deal with all of you for her by dragging you into the Underworld and killing you. You clearly survived that and then caught me and Athena unawares on the beach. Everything else, you're already aware of," Josephine finished, crossing her arms and staring defiantly at Brites. "I've got nothing else to offer you."

The room felt oppressive and heavy as she sat there, waiting for Brites to answer her. The Huntress' eyes bore into hers and a cruel smile danced on her lips. Josephine thought she looked like a wolf who'd finally cornered her prey. *I wonder if she's always been this way, or if that dead hero of hers turned her into this.* She was heartless, as nice as she appeared to be; cunning and vicious, as gentle as she portrayed herself.

"That's very enlightening," Brites finally said. Josephine did not release her breath, nor did her heart stop beating frantically. "But it's not enough. You're still withholding the information we're actually interested in, Josephine. I want details, the *exact* details of what Athena planned to do. Maybe you've been misunderstanding my question, so let me state it quite clearly: how was she going to invade Olympia?"

Josephine deliberated about whether there was any benefit to holding onto the information. Would it serve her better at a later date? When she could maybe bargain for something? But as she looked at Brites, she knew it wasn't worth trying.

I stand more to gain with the heroes, she decided. *There's nothing else I can hope to get from this.*

"There were two plans," Josephine said slowly, "that were supposed to be enacted at the same time. The Warriors were going to split into two groups: the first would serve as Athena's Honor Guard. They were going to march to Olympus and crown her. If she was sitting on Zeus' throne when the takeover happened, it would be nigh impossible to dethrone her. The Guard's role would be to help control the other gods, but Athena was sure that she could take on Zeus herself. It seemed unlikely that the other Olympians would put too much effort in defending Zeus. He's not well-liked as the king of the gods.

"The second contingent was going to be led by me. We

would come in from the South and sweep over Olympia. It hadn't been decided whether we'd attack each following one at a time, or whether I would split my contingent into divisions and we'd attack everyone simultaneously. Before I left, that seemed like the better option to us. Once the followings had been brought into submission, their gods would be forced to bend the knee to Athena. Naturally, we assumed there would be some kind of resistance amongst the gods and their followers, so many of our Warriors have been trained as infiltrators and spies that would keep them in check."

I've said so much at this point, Josephine thought to herself as she caught her breath, *what more could they ask for?*

"Is there anything else I can tell you?" she said aloud to Brites.

"No," Brites said after a drawn-out period of silence. She stood up again, drawing a long piece of rope from her pocket. "You're under arrest by the Olympian Council of Heroes. I'm taking you to Olympia so that we can present your information to the gods. You will need to testify again, but should you be found agreeable, I'm sure a deal about your life can be made."

Josephine balked. *Smart move, Brites.* It hadn't mattered whether she'd talked or not: her fate was not to be decided by the heroes, but by the gods. She'd thought that if she talked, they'd take into account everything they'd been through together, same as she had. But instead, she'd just played right into their hands. Perhaps the camaraderie she felt between them was a lie. Perhaps she was always going to be seen as the villain.

She offered no resistance as Brites tightly bound her hands. What was the point? The other heroes didn't even move as Brites secured her to be brought back. They stayed in their seats, silent and staring, though Josephine couldn't tell what they were thinking.

What a mess this is turning into.

CHAPTER 21
ATLANTIS

Day 17

"Poseidon, you cannot hide from us!" Zeus thundered, banging on the front gates to Atlantis. "We know you are sheltering your hero within these walls, and we will not abide by this clear violation of the laws of Olympia! She must be brought forth to trial as a madwoman. You cannot stand in the way of justice. Might I remind you that I am your king? You are bound to obey me!"

Wen-Tang watched from one of the upstairs windows as Zeus continued bellowing down at the entrance, ignored by everyone that was in the palace. She wasn't sure if the servants and diplomats were simply used to Zeus coming down and causing a ruckus from before the destruction, and therefore saw no reason to interfere, or if they were under strict orders from Poseidon not to let him in. She didn't particularly care about them, anyhow. Zeus was asking for her.

Not even asking, she thought. *He's demanding I surrender.*

She thought she could see why Zeus wanted her gone so much– why the gods had always been afraid of the heroes who went mad. She could feel the rage boiling underneath her skin constantly; driving her into a furious insanity where nothing mattered except the need for power, *any power, all power.* She would do anything for it. It was becoming harder and harder to fight off or ignore; the sensation kept pressing into her brain and bones. Wen-Tang was too tired to keep it at bay. All she wanted to do was surrender to the compulsions and let them sweep her away.

Maybe the gods were wise over the centuries, she thought. *Maybe they knew we wanted to be at rest from all of this.* She leaned her cheek against the cold window, turning her eyes away from Zeus to watch the fish swim by. She could hear his voice droning in the back of her mind, but she tried to tune it out. Lately, she had been too tired to do anything. Even wandering Atlantis held little of its previous charms. She spent most of her time now struggling to rise from a couch, or her spot by the window: either she was limp and exhausted, or so heady with rage that she couldn't move around a room safely. It was getting worse every day: Wen-Tang was beginning to long for the release of her service and the option to return to the mortal world and live the rest of her life in peace.

Poseidon is the one keeping me here, she thought to herself. *Against my will. I don't want to be in Atlantis anymore.*

The vague beginnings of a plan started to form in her mind. Her fingers absently drummed on the seashell-studded windowsill, and she twisted her head to observe the large room she lived in. A four-poster was in the center of it, with flowing blue curtains pulled closed to hide the mess of a bed she'd left. Desks, vanities, and dressers, all covered in various patterns of corals and shells, were scattered around to fill up the empty spaces. The walls were bare, for the most part, except for the climbing leaves of the potted algae and kelps that were tucked in the corners. It was a clean room, but clearly one that was rarely used: a guest's suite, Wen-Tang thought. She wondered why she didn't yet have a room of her own. And then her mind turned back to the plan at hand.

Poseidon didn't know what was good for her. That was clear enough to see. Not once had he come to visit since bringing her to Atlantis. The dull, constant pain of abandonment pierced Wen-Tang's heart once more. He didn't care that much about her; he had his own reasons for keeping her around. Zeus' offer to try her and send her home– so his still-continuing screams suggested– sounded more and more appealing. Perhaps she could slip out of the castle and surrender herself, bypassing Poseidon entirely. No one would try and stop her. They had no reason to.

Or, she could try and exact revenge on Poseidon for subjecting her to this. She could make her departure public and noted, let him watch her leave from his sequestered rooms, and be unable to do anything about it. Oh, how that would rankle him, after all the work he'd put in to bringing her back to Atlantis.

A devilish smile spread across her face. *I'll show him exactly what I'm like now and he'll have no choice but to agree to let me go. He'll see that I am too far gone and I will finally be at peace- I'll be free.* The boiling in her blood grew stronger as she dwelt on her goal. Maybe she wanted to fight Poseidon, duel him to the death to prove that she deserved her freedom. Or maybe she wanted his blood shed so that his ichor could be hers and she could become the goddess of the sea. Wen-Tang wasn't sure anymore. It all sounded equally delightful and horrible.

The unsettling weight of exhaustion pressed on her. *It's all too much work.* Even standing up took super-human effort now. If she had to guess, Wen-Tang thought the madness had more side effects than simply dangerous, uncontrollable emotion. It sapped at her own energy, in order to feed the godly blood pulsating under her skin. It was killing her from the inside.

They need to let me go.

She forced herself to stand up, all images of fighting Poseidon and triumphing leaving her mind. She struggled to stay on her feet. Stumbling through the room, she made her way down the stairs to one of the doors.

"Where are you going?" one of the servants asked, peering at her with a worried expression.

"Outside," Wen-Tang grumbled. "Not that it's any of your concern."

"I'm sorry, princess, very sorry, but we cannot let you go outside right now. I don't know if you noticed, but the Lord Zeus is out there. We're on strict orders from Poseidon that he isn't to see you. If you'll be begging my pardon, princess, let me escort you back to your room. You look dead tired."

"Don't stop me," Wen-Tang snarled, pulling her arm away when the servant reached towards her. "You won't tell me what to do! I'm in charge of you– and I order you to let me go outside. I intend to speak with Lord Zeus."

"Begging your pardon, princess, I really am, but I can't let you see him. Poseidon told us very clearly that Lord Zeus was trying to hurt you, princess, and we've all got a duty not to let that happen, of course. I'm very sorry, princess, I don't mean to make a fuss–"

Before she could grasp what was happening, Wen-Tang felt irritation take over her body and start controlling her every move. The warm flesh of the servant's skin squeezed between her fingers as Wen-Tang unwittingly tried to strangle her. She could see nothing, hear nothing, feel nothing. All that existed was the rage and the anger and it built up inside of her until it simply had to boil over in an explosion. She tossed the servant, barely breathing, onto the ground and stalked away towards the door, not caring whether she was still alive or not. Wen-

Tang stopped when she reached the doorknob. No one else had attempted to stop her or force her back, and the bubbling of her blood began to dissipate.

What am I doing? Why am I turning myself over to Zeus? I could kill him and become Queen of the Olympians.

I want to be freed from this. I don't want to go mad. Please, I don't want to go mad.

She turned the knob just as a flood of Poseidon's guards– as if they were alerted by her movements–came rushing down the stairs to stop her. *Where have they been this entire time?* She wondered. If they'd be tracking her, she hadn't noticed. But Wen-Tang was relatively certain there had been no guards watching over her: Poseidon's certainty that she wouldn't try to leave must have been too great.

Wen-Tang froze for a second, wondering if she should try and fight them. She decided against the idea. She fled outside, straight into the arms of Zeus. He looked down at her, confusion spreading across his face. In a moment, he realized who she was and saw the forces coming to pry her away. He wrapped an arm around her small body and vanished to Olympus, leaving the people of Atlantis far behind and below.

"I cannot simply send you back to the mortal world," Zeus frowned. "That is not within my powers to do, Wen-Tang. Without Poseidon releasing you from his service, it would not help you– you would still go mad. A trial must be convened, and Poseidon must be convinced to let you go. Until then, you're best staying in Olympus, where the other gods can keep an eye on you, should you need it."

Wen-Tang bowed her head, a sigh escaping her lips. They'd been going back and forth for an hour now, seated in uncomfortable marble chairs outside the temple complex. The sun beat down upon them, creating little drops of perspiration on her forehead, which trickled down into her eyes. Zeus seemed unaffected by the heat; the frown furrowed into his face was simply a result of her pleading to be let go.

"Is there no way you can make him come here quickly?" she asked. "I'm not in control of myself anymore, and I hate it–"

"I understand," Zeus said. "But that is the madness speaking. These sorts of things cannot be rushed. A summons has been sent for Poseidon and he will obey it sooner or later– maybe sooner, now that you are no longer in Atlantis. In the meantime, however, I'd like a report on the other heroes. The council has heard nothing from them since they left for the mortal world, and we worry that Athena will strike us without warning."

"I don't know what's happened since I left, obviously," Wen-Tang mumbled. "But I can tell you everything before that. We went from city to city, chasing the vague clues of Athena's whereabouts– Rome, Athens, Delphi– and Delphi is where things suddenly started to pick up. Hades has returned–"

Zeus nodded as if he already knew.

"Hades is back," Wen-Tang repeated. "And he's formed some kind of alliance with Athena because he tried to kill us on her behalf. He said only one of us would make it out alive–" the memory came flooding back to her, as if she had forgotten it entirely. "And that it would be Alexandria," she swallowed thickly. "I forgot that happened. Alexandria swears she didn't betray the heroes, but only passed along a message from Ares to Athena–"

"I shall speak to Ares," Zeus said, gravely. "I will not have traitors within my ranks."

"Anyway, we fell into the Underworld and barely made it back to the surface. Our exit led to the beaches off Thessaloniki– and that's where we finally ran into Athena and her hero, Josephine. We escaped that encounter, with Josephine captured. We've been using her for information since then– and then she told us about the madness."

A strained silence fell for a second as Wen-Tang collected herself. Zeus did not press her to continue.

"I knew I was going mad. I think Alexandria is, too. The others seem fine, at least for now, I guess. We discovered that the moly plant– Circe's plant– can protect the heroes from any interference from the gods. It can keep us from going insane, and it can keep the gods from erasing our memories and sending us back to the mortal world."

Zeus waved his hand, telling her to stop speaking.

"I know all of this. I received a message from Circe, who's been stabbed by one of your friends. They successfully collected their moly, it seems. It will not help them as much as they might think, however: the gods tried it long ago, with their first heroes. It might stave off the madness, but once the moly is lost, or dies, then the madness only takes on a more terrifying and fearful form."

"They stabbed Circe?" Wen-Tang exclaimed.

He nodded. "Alexandria, I believe. You're right. It seems the madness has gotten to her, too."

"What are you going to do about it, if she's got the moly?"

A thin smile crept up Zeus' lips. "That is for the king of the gods to know and for you to discover, Wen-Tang. Thank you for your story– do you have any other information concerning Athena? Have you managed to wring nothing out of Josephine?"

"Not before I left. I don't know what they're doing now," Wen-Tang replied. The heat beat into her brain, making her feel groggy and sleepy. All she wanted to do was lie down and sleep. Zeus appeared to notice her fatigue.

"Poseidon's magic is taking a toll on your body. You should rest now, Wen-Tang. Let me show you to the quarters where you'll be staying."

CHAPTER 22
OLYMPUS

Day 18

"The Olympians must be assembled immediately," Brites ordered the guards at the front of Olympus. The gold coating on everything glimmered in the light and overwhelmed Alexandria's senses; she was unable to take it all in in one go. Bright and yellow, gleaming with gems and marble, the palace was the epitome of godliness, she thought. Alexandria stood beside Brites, with Jasmin the pig tucked under her arm. They still had not found a remedy for her transformation and Alexandria could feel her squirming. *It must be stressful to be a pig.* Triniya and Josephine stood behind them, Josephine's hands bound tightly with rope.

The guard, dressed in the livery of the Sons of Justice, looked them over. "Come in," he bowed. "I will give your message to Lord Zeus immediately. He is in a meeting at the moment, but he will receive you shortly."

Brites strode in, leading the way to the empty throne room.

Alexandria looked up and admired the golden dome above her. Hammered into the soft metal were scenes from mythology: Artemis and the moon, Apollo and his golden chariot, Ares with her sword... There were others she could not decipher: plants and animals and birds flitting around the brilliant backdrops of wide plains and grass that seemed to undulate in the invisible wind. The room was massive, stretching on in glorious colours to the twelve thrones at the other end of it, all gold and bejeweled. The light from the windows bathed the whole place in warmth.

Every one of the thrones was empty, but Brites approached them and bowed, anyway. Alexandria copied her. They stood there, waiting.

"He'll be here soon, I'm sure," Brites said.

"If he could hurry, that would be great. I'm hungry," Triniya said.

"Now really isn't the time," Alexandria huffed.

"Heroes of Olympia!" Zeus thundered as he entered the room, the golden doors thudding against the walls. He was followed by Apollo, who looked harried and tired. Apollo's eyes roamed across the heroes, and his gaze widened when he saw Jasmin was missing. Then, when he saw the pig, he heaved a sigh. Zeus' eyes fell on Josephine immediately; his eyebrow rose with interest.

Alexandria watched as he settled on the throne and peered down at the heroes, like a statue, fixed and immobile in its gaze. The greetings between the other heroes and him slipped by her ears unheard; she was so focused on trying to read the minute lines of his face. They revealed nothing about what he was thinking. He studiously avoided her eye contact, Alexandria thought, seemingly only interested in Josephine.

I guess that makes sense, she thought.

"This must be Athena's hero," Zeus finally interrupted Brites, who was still relating some small anecdote or other. "I have just heard the full story of your travels, Brites, forgive me if I have no interest in listening to it again. How long has Josephine been under your care?"

Brites' brow furrowed in confusion. "Several days, I think. We ran into a couple issues during the trip and that is what delayed us, my Lord."

Alexandria saw a flash of lightning in the god's eyes. Though he did not appear angry, she could see the rippling effect in his face. Her own rage bubbled up to the surface, tensing her chest and settling into her heart. If Zeus made a threatening move, she would stop him. Her heart raced with the *thud, thud, thud* of fear and excitement. She wanted to pull out her sword. She wanted blood.

And as soon as it came, the feeling dissipated. Alexandria felt around in her pocket, clutching tightly at the moly buried at the very bottom. She fingered the crumpling, drying plant, willing it to work. *If only Wen-Tang had hung on for a little bit longer,* she thought. *She could have gotten the help I'm getting now. Assuming the moly's working.*

"Do not lie to me, Brites, Huntress of Artemis. I do not take kindly to false heroes– I know that you abandoned your quest to stop Athena."

Alexandria watched Brites' cheeks whiten. *She looks ill.* The realization overtook her: the harshness of Brites' treatment of Josephine had nothing to do Sophia or with her fears for Olympia. She had kept it better hidden than Wen-Tang or Alexandria had, but Brites was suffering from the same disease. *She's going mad, too.*

Alexandria craned her neck to look at Triniya. Were they all? *How are Triniya and Jasmin still okay? They've been heroes a lot longer than the rest of us. What powers do they have that no one else does?*

"In fact, I recently heard from Circe, who is recovering from a wound inflicted by one of you." Zeus rose. Alexandria stared at him; he was taller than when he came in. He appeared to have grown in stature. "I know you have moly plants, all of you. I also know that some of you are teetering on the edge of madness. Where is Wen-Tang, Poseidon's hero?"

There was no answer.

"We will discuss this when the council of gods assembles. I have already summoned them. Since none of you are aware of this, Wen-Tang is here as well, and her fate will be decided during the council– she has requested to be released from service and sent back to the mortal world. The moly does not protect you the way you think it does," Zeus continued, "but as I said, that is for later. At the moment, I am far more interested in Athena. That is a pressing threat to Olympia and with the war against the North Guard still raging on, we are left vulnerable to an outside attack."

Triniya frowned. "I thought that the war was over."

Zeus shrugged. "It is nearing its end– but there remains pesky resistance to the demands of the gods."

Jasmin oinked. Zeus averted his eyes. Alexandria watched with interest as he did. *Is he not going to change her back?*

Apollo frowned. He waved his hand and Jasmin once again became a human. She collapsed with relief into Alexandria's arms. Alexandria patted her back gingerly, more interested in Zeus' shifting eyes than in a god fixing Jasmin's curse. Zeus stretched his arm forth, and then, as if changing his mind, he dropped it and moved forward.

"I'm a human again," Jasmin whispered to Alexandria. "Oh thank the gods. I can't tell you how absolutely horrible being a pig was; that was terrible."

"Jasmin, shh," Alexandria hissed. Her patience was wearing down with every second. *Zeus knows that Brites and I are going mad. What's he going to do about it? I need to know–*

"Sorry," Jasmin's eyebrows scrunched. "I didn't mean to–"

"Not now! We can talk about it later," Alexandria mumbled. "Not the time."

Triniya overheard them and frowned. *She's mad at me about Jasmin, too. I cannot get a break,* Alexandria thought bitterly. *It's not my fault! I don't have time to deal with this right now! I'm going crazy and I don't know what's going to happen!*

Zeus took a step forward towards Josephine, his eyes sparking with anger. "What is your goddess planning?"

Josephine straightened her back. Alexandria saw her eyes flit nervously towards Brites and then her face steeled itself.

"I will grant you a deal, Josephine. I am not in the habit of disposing of other gods' heroes, nor do I have the purview to release you from Athena's service. Whether I wish it or not, you are one of the heroes of the Olympians. However, be warned, that I have the power to make your life in Olympia truly miserable. I can torture you for the rest of your service until you are begging to be released. It is in your best interests to cooperate, Josephine. If you do, perhaps I will be clement with you. Should you refuse, there are many prisons under this temple and Athena's hero need not make public appearances..."

"You have to promise me that I will be given a seat on the council. And accorded all of the honours of a hero," Josephine said. "Then, I'll tell you everything I know."

"I can accord that," Zeus agreed.

"And you have to protect me from Athena's anger."

"You are a shrewd hero. Looking out for yourself and your own interests. I cannot stand between you and your goddess, but I may be able to persuade Athena to one direction or the other. However, she has not been invited to the council so you will not have to face her now. Until she should return to Olympia humbly and with no ill intention, you may serve me and the council of gods. Do these terms suit you?"

Josephine nodded quickly, a flicker of relief in her eyes.

Alexandria stifled a yawn as Josephine began her entire story over again.

Zeus nodded along through the entirety of it, but Apollo seemed not to notice anything that was happening. His mind was clearly somewhere else. Alexandria wondered what he was thinking about: if his mind was dwelling on Jasmin and wondering if she was going mad like everyone else.

"You have proven yourself enlightening," Zeus finally said to Josephine, once her story was concluded. Alexandria blinked. *It's already over?* "We will launch an invasion into the mortal world before Athena has a chance to get a hold of Olympia. If there must be a battle against her, it ought to be the mortal world, for we do not care about what happens to it."

What? Alexandria thought. *We don't care about the mortal world?*

"I thought we were supposed to protect the mortal world," Triniya interrupted.

"Perhaps," Zeus brushed her comment aside. "But it must also serve our purposes. I can always change the memories of the mortals to disguise this war."

At that comment, it seemed like the room exploded with arguments about memory, madness, moly, and the control of the gods.

CHAPTER 23
OLYMPUS

Day 19

"Silence!" Zeus ordered, his voice ringing out through the room. All of the heroes snapped their mouths shut, hearing the threat in his tone. The doors swung open as his last syllables died out and a stream of deities flowed in.

When the throne room filled with gods, it became more than magnificent. It became horrifying. The power radiating from the Olympians pulsed through the room, sending shockwaves through Alexandria's chest. Each one hurt more than the last until they were almost unbearable. But she gritted her teeth and bore it, her head unbowed. There was no reason to make them suspicious that she was mad. They were all a little fragile and clearly struggling under the weight of their titles and powers, but none of them were dangerous yet.

Zeus' tongue is made of honey, but I don't believe a single word he said. He doesn't have the best interest of the heroes at hand, I'm sure of that, Alexandria thought, looking up at him. There he sat, in all of his regal splendor, discussing some triviality with Ares, who was at his right hand. The goddess had not deigned to look at her hero since she'd arrived and Alexandria could feel the pulsating displeasure of her goddess, though she was not sure what for. Was it because she had not aided Athena behind the backs of the other heroes? Was it because Ares could tell that Alexandria's strength was fading in the face of insanity? Or had it to do with the failure to complete the mission they'd set out to do? Like always, Alexandria found herself grasping for an explanation for Ares' behaviour and being unable to come up with one.

"Heroes of Olympia," Zeus began. "You have appeared before us today, guilty of failing in your task. You brought back Athena's hero, but not Athena, and have no concrete evidence of her plans, besides the mere words of Josephine, who might be lying to us all. Furthermore, you abandoned your mission in order to search for the moly plant– so that you might defy the customs of Olympia and the rulings of the gods through your own power. In doing this, you mortally wounded the Lady Circe. Have I forgotten any other misdemeanors?"

Alexandria's jaw dropped. *That is not what happened... we just told him everything, and he'd promised... Zeus lied to us,* she thought. *He lied to us!*

Her blood boiled and her eyes clouded over. She breathed in and out, trying to calm herself down. The other heroes were silent, crushed under the weight of all of these accusations, too shocked at Zeus' blatant lies to speak. Alexandria twisted her hands together to try to ground herself. Even worse than listening to Zeus speak was feeling his gaze, constant and inescapable.

"You have betrayed your task and Olympia; you must suffer the appropriate punishment now. You are no longer to be heroes of Olympus. The madness has taken Wen-Tang–"

Poseidon bristled and fumed. "Where is she?" he demanded.

Zeus held up a hand. "In time, brother. She has agreed to renounce her position and return to the mortal world, as she should. You will do nothing to stop her." Zeus' eyes flashed. Alexandria caught the glimmer of deep-seated rage in them, rage that would not be halted, though it was being controlled for the moment.

Poseidon deflated at his brother's words and sunk back into his seat.

Zeus cleared his throat and continued. "I will keep my promise to you, Josephine; but you will be a prisoner of war until your goddess has been apprehended– fear not, you will retain your honor and your title, but you will not be free to do whatever you wish in this country."

Josephine's face contorted and her muscles tensed. Alexandria felt her heart beating wilder. *He lied to her too. She's not going to take this well.*

"I am being clement," Zeus said. "And I will brook no disagreement with that. You are welcome, of course, to refuse my offer and to languish in prison, Josephine. But– as for you other heroes, I am not so merciful anymore." He peered down at them. Alexandria shivered; she felt as if he were reading her, piercing through all of her thoughts, like he could sense the madness growing inside of her and would tease out to expose her to the other heroes.

"Wen-Tang is not the only one among you who has gone mad," he said. "Alexandria... Brites... step forward."

Alexandria rooted her feet to the ground and refused to move, lifting her chin to face the god. *I saw how scared Athena was of Wen-Tang when she revealed herself. I can scare the gods just as easily– I will not be taken. I will not have my memory wiped. I will not be returned to the mortal world, disgraced and disowned by the gods. I haven't been here that long! I can't be finished yet! My adventure's only just begun! And I will not cower to the king of the gods while he sits on his throne of lies.*

She felt the weight of the gazes of the other heroes, as they swiveled their heads to look at her and Brites.

"I'm not leaving Olympia," she announced, her voice loud and strong. Her sword left its place at her side, shining in her tight grasp, held up for all the gods to see. "You can't make me."

"Alexandria," Ares said, warily watching the sword. "You are merely proving that you are too dangerous to be left loose... you cannot threaten the gods."

Alexandria's eyes burned with anger. "You invited me here, made me your hero, and now you're ready to betray me– just like that! Just because I have grown more powerful and more capable. I can serve you now better than ever!"

"You don't know what you're saying..." Ares shook her head.

"You cannot reason with madness," Zeus interrupted. "Cease this pointless conversation. Alexandria has proven herself too volatile to be left in Olympia."

"I didn't think it would be possible for someone to lose control so quickly," Apollo interjected, pointedly looking at Zeus, as if he knew something, his brows furrowed. "She's new to Olympia, Zeus; she hasn't even been a hero for a year... why on earth would it have happened so quickly?" His question would have more merit if he also pointed out Zeus' lie to the other gods... but he didn't say anything more. Rage burned in Alexandria's chest.

"I think we're all wondering that," Hermes frowned. "Why haven't Triniya and Jasmin exhibited any symptoms? They've been heroes far longer."

"It has to do with the strength of the hero in question," Hestia said softly. "Nothing more, nothing less. Those that believe more strongly in the gods and more deeply in their position are less susceptible to madness... not entirely, of course, but it certainly slows down the process. Unfortunately,

Wen-Tang has been a hero for a long time now, and it seems her tolerance has waned. As for Alexandria and Brites, they were clearly not of the right beliefs to succeed as a hero." She turned to the girls in question. "I am sorry, my dears, that we brought you here at all. You were never meant for it, that I can see now."

Alexandria's free hand balled into a fist. Her heart pounded in her ears. *How dare they– they brought me here and gave me a title and a place amongst the Amazons, and now they want to take it all away, just like that! It's not fair- I won't do it!*

Before she knew what was happening, she stepped up to Ares' throne and held her sword to the goddess' throat.

Ares' eyes widened. "Alexandria," she whispered. "What are you doing?"

"You can't make me leave," Alexandria snarled. Her hands shook but she did not move the sword away; rather, she pressed it harder, drawing a thin drip of ichor. Ares let out a small gasp. Her eyes turned red, deep, dark, and fuming. Alexandria met her gaze, her mouth drawn into a hard line.

I will not leave without a fight, she decided.

Ares retaliated by pushing Alexandria off of her, standing up, and pulling out her own sword. The other heroes immediately gathered around their own, with flashing steel and dangerous glints in their eyes; the gods raised themselves from their thrones and descended the steps to meet their heroes, trying to appease them, to make them put down their weapons.

But Alexandria and Brites, their anger riled and the hazy feelings of the madness taking over, led a charge, ignoring the voices of reason on both sides. Alexandria found herself facing Ares first. Her vision was so tunneled that she could not see what any of the other heroes were doing, but she did not care. *The gods will pay for what they've done to me. I will hold them responsible,* she thought to herself. *I will not be discarded so easily.*

She slammed her sword and body against the goddess, who

pushed her off and raised her own sword to Alexandria's arm. The hero ducked and struck against Ares' feet, cutting against her left ankle. Ares howled and brought the flat of her blade down against her hero's head. Alexandria let out a cry of pain and lunged between the goddess' legs, raising herself to face Ares' back, but the goddess turned, and their swords met once again in a flash of light and clashes of steel. They battled, evenly matched for a time, as their feet danced and their swords flew to the right, to the left, each backing up and advancing in turn. Alexandria's arms began to tire; the feeling of weariness settled over her, but the sinking of her body only angered her more.

With renewed determination, as if she were rabid, Alexandria struck against Ares. Her strokes became shorter and more tense; she stopped lengthening her blows or reaching with the tip of her sword. Instead, she tried to overwhelm Ares with the sheer number of blows she struck. But the faster she moved, the sloppier they became. Before she could understand what had happened, her sword flew across the room, steel pressed against her chest, and her hands were in the air.

"Surrender," Ares ordered.

Alexandria's anger dissipated into her veins, and suddenly, she felt weak and woozy, as if she'd expended all of the energy in her bones. Her eyes felt fuzzy, and her focus shifted in and out. For a brief second, Alexandria thought she might become too tired to stand. She wondered if she might faint. But the moment passed; her mind cleared. Ares came back into focus. She felt the cold steel against her hot, flushed skin and she shuddered inadvertently. She gazed around the room. Apollo was standing in front of Jasmin, his hand held out towards her. She took it, and he pulled her into a hug, shielding her from the disaster around them. His golden cloaks and layers protected her. Alexandria flinched at the image, thinking of the differences between her and Jasmin.

He cares for her as his own. I wonder if that's why she hasn't gone mad. Because her god is not using her or extending her beyond her means. He nurtures and cares for her— and Hestia cares for Triniya in the same way.

The idea grew in her mind. As she thought about it, Alexandria became more convinced that it must have something to do with that. *Wen-Tang only began to go mad after Poseidon made her the heir to Atlantis– used her to continue his dynasty. Brites began to go mad when she replaced Sophia because Artemis needed someone, anyone, to do it and didn't care who it was. The sword of Penthesilea probably sped up my madness.*

No wonder Triniya and Jasmin are okay.

I wonder if the gods know.

I wonder if they know what makes this happen.

Zeus pinned Brites to a column with her own sword, and just like that, as abruptly as it had begun, the skirmish in the throne room was over. In a swift motion, Ares dropped her sword and tied Alexandria's hands together with rope that she conjured out of nowhere. Zeus did the same with Brites; Alexandria saw her wince as the rope dug into her wrists. Her own bonds were also uncomfortably tight. *It makes sense though. Atar scared them. They won't take risks with us.*

The two of them were led to the middle of the room and the gods returned to their thrones. An oppressive silence hung over the room; it almost seemed sacrilegious to breathe. Zeus sat there, his breath held, until the doors cracked open one more time.

Alexandria heard Jasmin gasp behind her. Triniya let out a small cry. Brites inhaled sharply and Alexandria craned her neck around to look, her heart pounding out of her chest. There stood Wen-Tang, her captain's hat cocked on her straight black hair, her eyes narrowed at the two heroes, tied up, in the middle of the room. Her eyes were dull and lifeless, but there was an air of peace around her.

"Lord Zeus," she greeted him with a bow, pointedly ignoring Poseidon, who gasped and tried to stand up from his throne but found himself unable to. He turned red and blustering, accused Zeus of using his powers to keep him from standing.

"If you can't behave civilly," Zeus shrugged, "I will be forced to take other means. I will not allow you to harass your hero. She has made her decision; she has agreed to return to the mortal world because she has recognized that her madness cannot be cured otherwise. I will not allow you to dissuade her."

Poseidon ignored him. He turned his attention to Wen-Tang.

"Wen-Tang, listen to me... return with me to Atlantis. I will find a way to make you better, I will. I know it's never been done before but we can discover it. The power of Atlantis will stabilize you, I know it will–"

Alexandria heard the false ring in his voice. She knew Wen-Tang recognized it too. *He cannot fix this. It cannot be fixed.* Her eyes met with those of Ares, who almost seemed to be looking through her. *She would never offer to fix me.*

If she couldn't be a good hero, Ares no longer cared. There was no warm, familiar relationship between them. They were a god and a hero, nothing more, nothing less. *Ares would never be wishy-washy for me.*

Alexandria realized she respected that. And as soon as she did, she felt the madness rear up in the back of her head. Her eyes went dark and fuzzy again and she found herself gasping for air, desperately trying to break through her bonds.

In the blink of an eye, Zeus was by her side. His warm head rested on the top of her head.

"Breathe, Alexandria. You will be released from this soon," he whispered. He sounded gentle, a far cry from the cold, angry god of a few moments earlier. Her mind felt like a flurry of confused emotions: desperation to be released from the sensations overwhelming her, desire to act upon the destructive anger she felt, reassurance at Zeus's promise, anger at him for making her mad and for lying about them to the other gods.

She could barely hear Zeus address the others in the room.

"The moly might staunch the madness temporarily," he told the heroes. "But it does not save you from it. It is the curse of Olympia, which is not made for heroes. Demigods were safe from this madness because they shared our own blood. But heroes are simple mortals... you are not meant for the power we bestow upon you. If there were another way, we would try that. But alas, you must sacrifice some of yourself for us. Wen-Tang, Brites, Alexandria... you have served us faithfully and well, for as long as you have been able to. But it is time to give up your titles and return to the mortal world before you destroy yourselves entirely."

Wen-Tang's spine straightened, and she squared her shoulders. "I am ready. I don't want to suffer this anymore. I want to be released."

Poseidon choked, but no words came from him. Finally, with great difficulty, he managed to say: "Then I will release you."

Alexandria leaned her head against Zeus' chest and felt the warmth flow from his body to her head, silencing the noise in her mind. The relief was overwhelming. She had not realized how painful and noisy her thoughts had become until they were silent and still, and she could see clearly what the madness had done to her.

"I want it to stop," she whispered.

"We will release you," Zeus promised. He pulled away from her. A tear slipped down Alexandria's cheek. *Josephine and Triniya and Wen-Tang were wrong. The gods don't erase our memories or send us back out of meanness or anger. They are doing their best to help us, mend us after breaking us.*

It's still all their faults.

But I want to go back home.

Sudden longing overtook her. She missed Carmen and her parents and the life she'd left behind in the mortal world. She wanted to go hiking and to be free of the worry of leading armies or negotiating between gods.

"I want to go home," she said aloud.

Brites was the only one of the heroes who held out.

"I will go to the mortal world," she said reluctantly. "On one condition."

"You are not in a position to be making demands," Zeus pointed out, but Brites stood firm.

"You claim you're doing this for our own good, Lord Zeus, but you informed none of us of these dangers before taking us on as heroes. I will go to the mortal world and to a regular life, if you swear an oath to inform heroes of the dangers of the role before offering it to them."

The gods murmured to each other, too low for Alexandria to pick out any meaning.

"Brites makes an excellent point," Hestia said finally. "We have not properly warned our heroes of the dangers of their task. We have taken advantage of them, even if we did not mean to."

"Very well," Zeus turned to Brites and nodded. "We will assent to that request."

"I have one more," Brites added.

Zeus' cheeks turned pink, and he appeared to be holding back an outburst of anger. Alexandria winced. *Don't push it, Brites.*

"What is it?" Hestia answered in Zeus' stead. "If it is fair, we will consider it."

"Give the heroes the moly we collected," Brites said. "Let them hold onto it and slow the process of their madness, so they can stay here as long as they can. Only when it becomes dangerous– then bring them back to the mortal world."

Zeus' shoulders dropped; he shook his head but assented. "Very well. That also seems fair. But you may ask no more favours of us, Brites."

Once again, he addressed everyone in general. "We have delayed long enough. Heroes, you have served us well and for your loyalty, we thank you. The Council of the Olympians releases you of your service. Return to your homes in the mortal world and find peace there. You will not remember your time here so that you do not long for it. But rest assured, your names will remain in the annals of Olympia."

A strange, warm tingling overtook Alexandria...

THE END

Acknowledgments

The Owl's Eye was a difficult book to write. It seemed at every turn that the characters were trying to thwart me and I had no idea where the plot was going. It was a new feeling for me, because both *Olympia* and *The North Guard* seemed to flow easily and I don't remember many issues with them. At times, I certainly felt discouraged and unsure about the entire *Chronicles of Chaos* series. But, somehow, it did manage to get written and it ended up being my (possibly) new favorite in the series. I always enjoy giving different characters a time to shine in each new book, and exploring Wen-Tang's personality was great fun. I love a good pirate!

As always, there are so many people who went into the making of this book. First and foremost, my fiance, Daxxton, who spent many hours walking with me and talking about the plot holes with me. Ultimately, a lot of this story came from him: when I had no idea where it was going, he provided me with brilliant ideas. I am so fortunate to have him by my side. His entire family's support has been a great blessing: thank you, Kim, Leslie, Larkkin, and Gaige. My own family's rave reviews about the previous books have also warmed my heart immensely and helped me persevere through this next one, especially Karl's suggestions on what I should include and Thomas' vocal love for the stories. I hope someday I'll get to read their books. And thank you to Aml and Reese for good friendship and conversation, that made sure I didn't get stuck in Olympia.

The SnowRidge team continues to blow me away: Savanna and her wonderful, insightful edits; who worked with me over several drafts of this book and handled with grace all of the delays on my end. Bryce, who handles all of the business aspects of this process, which is great, because I don't have a head for numbers. Hanah, whose help with my series has been invaluable. And thank you, Sarah, my wonderful cover artist, who did the art for all three of my books. You exceed every single one of my expectations, every time, and really bring the characters to life. I am so lucky that you agreed to work with me!

And finally, thank you to everyone who left reviews or commented on *Olympia* and *The North Guard*: I appreciate you so much. It's so special to know that I'm building up a little readership slowly, and that people are enjoying my writing. I have poured over those reviews countless times and they have reminded me why I decided to write in the first place. I love sharing the world and characters of Olympia with you and I feel very blessed to have been given the opportunity. I hope you find *The Owl's Eye* an exciting adventure, and that it leaves you hungry for more!

ABOUT THE AUTHOR

Eva Grace is a full-time student and the author of "Red of Roses and Blood" from the anthology *Twisted Grimms*.

She has also contributed poetry to several publications including Calliope, Blank Spaces, and Bridge Ink.

You can find her on Instagram at @evagracewrites.

Made in the USA
Columbia, SC
27 March 2025

55739078R00133